PUF

'Quick! Turn on the news! Now!' Gran said. There was something in her voice – perhaps the high-pitched scream – that suddenly commanded everyone's attention.
'Why?' queried Mark.
'Because it's the end of the world!' Gran said.

The year is 2347. Every living thing has to move to a new planet. But along the way, the *Dogstar* – a Space Ark filled with all the world's canines – goes missing.

The Clark kids set out on a brave quest to rescue their beloved pet, Hobart. But with an evil genius and a rock-throwing alien tribe pitted against them, will they ever find him?

Based on episodes of Dogstar *written by Doug MacLeod and Philip Dalkin from the Media World Pictures TV series devised by Doug MacLeod, Colin South & John Tatoulis.*

PHILIP DALKIN

PUFFIN

PUFFIN BOOKS

Published by the Penguin Group
Penguin Books Ltd, 80 Strand, London WC2R 0RL, England
Penguin Group (USA) Inc., 375 Hudson Street, New York, New York 10014, USA
Penguin Group (Canada), 90 Eglinton Avenue East, Suite 700, Toronto, Ontario, Canada M4P 2Y3
(a division of Pearson Penguin Canada Inc.)
Penguin Ireland, 25 St Stephen's Green, Dublin 2, Ireland (a division of Penguin Books Ltd)
Penguin Group (Australia), 250 Camberwell Road, Camberwell, Victoria 3124, Australia
(a division of Pearson Australia Group Pty Ltd)
Penguin Books India Pvt Ltd, 11 Community Centre, Panchsheel Park, New Delhi – 110 017, India
Penguin Group (NZ), 67 Apollo Drive, Rosedale, North Shore 0632, New Zealand
(a division of Pearson New Zealand Ltd)
Penguin Books (South Africa) (Pty) Ltd, 24 Sturdee Avenue, Rosebank, Johannesburg 2196, South Africa

Penguin Books Ltd, Registered Offices: 80 Strand, London WC2R 0RL, England

puffinbooks.com

First published by Penguin Group (Australia),
a division of Pearson Australia Group Pty Ltd, 2007
Published in Great Britain in Puffin Books 2009
1

Text copyright © Philip Dalkin, 2007
Cover design © Scott Vanden Bosch, 2007
Text design by Adam Laszczuk © Penguin Group (Australia), 2007
All rights reserved

The moral right of the author has been asserted

Set in Stone Serif and Zemke Hand
Made and printed in England by Clays Ltd, St Ives plc

Except in the United States of America, this book is sold subject to the condition
that it shall not, by way of trade or otherwise, be lent, re-sold, hired out, or otherwise
circulated without the publisher's prior consent in any form of binding or cover other
than that in which it is published and without a similar condition including this
condition being imposed on the subsequent purchaser

British Library Cataloguing in Publication Data
A CIP catalogue record for this book is available from the British Library

ISBN: 978–0–141–32446–3

www.greenpenguin.co.uk

Penguin Books is committed to a sustainable future
for our business, our readers and our planet.
The book in your hands is made from paper
certified by the Forest Stewardship Council.

For Henry, James and Emily

MORAY COUNCIL LIBRARIES & INFO.SERVICES	
20 26 36 10	
Askews	
JC	

At around ten minutes past two on December the fifteenth of the year 2344, Grandma Clark brought a soft, round bundle of fur into the Clark household. She placed it gently on the floor of the lounge. Two shining eyes stared back at her. Her son, Mark Clark, was angered by this seemingly innocent act.

'I thought I'd made it very clear – crystal clear – abundantly clear – no pets,' said Mark, father of the house.

Mark had never liked dogs or cats. He detested budgerigars of all shapes and colours. He particularly loathed goldfish. No reason – just hated them. And for some unexplained reason, he was intensely repulsed by possums. The very thought of them licking their fur or nibbling fruit created uncomfortable sensations in Mark that he could never satisfactorily explain.

'They just make me sick,' Mark would proclaim (or exclaim or declaim) – and that would be the end of it.

No matter that it was a tiny and seemingly harmless puppy, the presence of this animal really got under his skin. Even though his kids had been pleading for a pet for as long as he could remember, Mark stood firm.

'It can't stay here. No way. Not possible,' said Mark.

'Ohhh . . .' replied Gran, 'I must have misunderstood.'

We could probably talk a lot here about Gran's tactics. Was she genuinely vague – truly a bit dim – or was this a craftily contrived act? Who knows? Does it really matter? As it transpired, at two twenty-five p.m., Mark's wife Greta came home to find Mark happily romping alone with the puppy – trying to teach it 'fetch'.

Mark looked up self-consciously. 'Er . . . it's for the kids . . .' he stammered.

By three fifteen, when the children had returned from school, he was proudly introducing them to their new family pet. 'Look at those eyes – you can tell he's smart. Look at that tail wag!'

'He's beautiful,' said Simone, the eldest and most thoughtful of the Clark children.

'He certainly is a most visually appealing canine specimen,' observed Lincoln – at two years old, the youngest, smartest and easily the most articulate.

Silence.

'What's for dinner?' said Glenn, the middle child.

Simone, Glenn and Lincoln bonded immediately with the puppy.

'He likes me best!' Glenn boasted as he slipped him a slice of chicken loaf from the fridge.

'He likes chicken meat,' Simone responded, drily.

'He no doubt likes whatever he's fed as he really hasn't had enough life-experience to determine particular favourites at this point in time,' said Lincoln.

Again, silence.

'Uhh . . . yeah, right, Linc,' said Mark with his customary eloquence. 'Hey . . . here's a thought. What will we call him?'

'Barry!' was Simone's suggestion – after the famous twenty-second-century politician, perhaps.

'Killer!' offered Gran.

'Meteor Boy,' shouted Glenn – a reference to his hero Planet Man's teenage sidekick.

'Is "Butch" too . . . ?' mused Greta, before being cut off.

Mark had interrupted with, 'What about "Mark" – no, wait – that won't work . . .'

'I have an idea . . . a suggestion . . .' said Lincoln.

Now, it was generally accepted that Lincoln's ideas were worth listening to. And once listened to, it was usually wise to adopt them. So when the other Clarks realized that Lincoln was about to propose a name, they listened in respectful silence – knowing what was coming was going to be good.

'Hobart,' said Lincoln, simply.

The other Clarks exchanged looks.

Mark and Greta nodded at their smartest child.

Gran patted Lincoln on the head.

Simone smiled.

Glenn took a bite of chicken meat.

At that exact moment, the puppy barked. A joyous yelp that was the first sound he'd made so far.

'He's saying he approves and he's very happy to be here with us – so "Hobart" it is,' said Simone.

Now you know. That's where it began – Simone's habit

of interpreting Hobart's barks, growls and groans, and translating them into English. In fact, she was almost always completely wrong. Hobart's thoughts were quite different.

The small puppy no-hairs must be part of the rest of this pack.

Are they going to sniff my crumper? No. They're ruffing me. They really should sniff my crumper. I want to sniff theirs but they keep holding me and ruffing me. How can you say 'hello' properly if you don't sniff crumpers?

They smell . . . well . . . they smell different. But they like me. They must like me, they're rubbing me now. That's good. Ohhh . . . scratch my tummy. Ohhhh . . . that's even better. More. Oh yeah . . . the ears . . . like that. Yes. Mmmmmmm.

Over the years Hobart grew into a mid-sized dog with browny tones. He had that 'everydog' quality – you could never quite pick which breed he was. Glenn would often let Hobart lick his hand. Sometimes a thought would bubble up.

'See that, Simone? He likes me better than you.'

'Huh! Hobart – give me paw.' Simone held out her hand. They bumped knuckles, rolled wrists, touched middle fingers, high-fived each other, then rubbed noses. All in sync, all timed to perfection. Glenn rolled his eyes. 'See that?' said Simone. 'He likes me better than you.'

Then Lincoln, by now five years old, stepped forward. 'Observe. Hobart – rotate laterally and feign rigor mortis.' Right on cue, Hobart rolled over and played dead. 'I think it's blatantly obvious that I am Hobart's most-favoured sibling,' Lincoln observed.

Glenn was peeved – as he had been since Lincoln spoke his first word at the tender age of three weeks (for the record, it was 'photosynthesis'). 'Why do you always have to use so many big words, Lincoln?' he asked.

'It's relative, Glenn. I have a universally recognized genius intellect and you are an arboreal primate.'

'Eh?'

'He means you're a monkey, Glenn,' said Simone.

'Oh.'

Later, at the dinner table, picking at a genetically modified banana (it was considered lucky to get a bent one), Glenn was still pondering whether he'd been insulted. On the table next to him was his Planet Man action figure.

In a moment of clarity, Glenn suddenly looked from the banana to the figurine. He smiled.

'Look, Planet Man! This banana is the same shape as a Karzorkian Deep-Space Stealth Fighter!' He buzzed the banana around Planet Man's head like a dive-bomber. Planet Man's eyes lit up in a pre-programmed response to the sound of Glenn's voice. Its head swivelled to face Glenn. Its mouth opened.

'A good crime fighter – *Glenn* – eats from all five food groups every day,' said the doll. It finished with a brisk, military-style salute. Glenn smiled.

Simone rolled her eyes. Planet Man's verbal responses were always a little disappointing. The 'Glenn' always sounded a little discordant, tonally different to the rest of his pre-recorded answer. Still, Glenn never seemed to mind.

'Do you have to have your doll at the table?' said Simone, testily.

'It's not a doll! It's an action figurine!' said Glenn. 'And, as such, it should be treated with respect.'

Mark opened his mouth, but Greta got in first. 'Mark – I think it's best that we don't stifle the children.'

Mark thought about this. He had no idea what Greta meant, but he knew it was probably best to say nothing. So he went back to eating dinner. As usual, all the food on the table was genetically modified, synthetically derived garbo-hydrates. It looked exactly like twenty-first-century food, only much more colourful.

Lincoln ate slowly and stared thoughtfully out the thirty-third-floor window of the Clarks' dining room. Outside, hundreds of identical tower buildings stretched into the gloomy, smog-filled evening as far as he could see – which wasn't far because of the gloomy, smog-filled evening. Huge plasma screens glowed eerily through the haze, making it pulse with bright colours. The products being advertised meant little to Lincoln. High above them was another glow. The now permanent half-moon hung limply in the sky, casting a feeble light over the endless metropolis below. Technically, today would be listed as a 'Full Moon', but unrestricted lunar mining for the alloy Dalkinite (the densest material in the universe) had removed the moon's entire western hemisphere.

As Lincoln stared out, flying craft of all types sped by at the higher levels. Below them, a sea of jetestrians – all using jet-packs to get around – zipped past the grime-covered window. Nobody looked at each other as they passed.

The lower levels were mercifully lost from sight in a cocktail of seething, bubbling industrial pollutants – a heady mixture of toxic chemicals and gases still quaintly referred to as smog – but, really, it was best not to think about it too much. Below that . . . well, let's not go there, either.

'Dad?' said Glenn. 'Did the sky used to be blue once?'

'That's just a myth, Glenn. It's always been a nice brown colour. Just like the pure, fresh water we drink.'

Mark toasted his eloquence by raising his glass. He took a sip of the semi-transparent liquid, winced, then set it down again.

'I read in a book that the sky used to be blue,' said Glenn.

'Amazing,' said Simone.

'I thought so.'

'No – amazing you read a book.'

'Dad! Simone's being mean to me again!'

'Simone,' said Mark, trying to sound authoritative, 'don't pick on people who aren't as smart as you.' Then, quickly realizing he might have said something stifling, he looked to Greta. Greta returned the look with – 'the look'.

Simone smiled to herself and lowered a piece of genetically modified veal substitute (actually a soy/kelp/ cardboard derivative) below the table to Hobart. He swallowed it eagerly.

At that very moment, Gran ran into the room. 'Quick! Turn on the news! Now!' she said. There was something in her voice – perhaps the high-pitched scream – that suddenly commanded everyone's attention.

'Why?' queried Mark.

'Because it's the end of the world!'

Simone scrambled for the remote control to the USI ('Ultra Super Infranet') screen. She hit the play button. The tiny holographic projector on the wall shone suddenly and a 3-D image grew in front of them until it covered the entire wall.

The ludicrously handsome news presenter, Hank Henry, was on screen. As usual, he was smiling his benign, slightly patronizing smile from behind his garish news desk.

'. . . world leaders revealed today that owing to centuries of pollution, the Earth will become uninhabitable on Tuesday at three-thirty p.m. – Eastern Standard Time . . .'

The rest of the news story faded into the background as the Clark family absorbed the ghastly reality of what they were hearing.

Glenn was perplexed. 'Uninhabitable – is that bad?'

'It's very bad,' said Lincoln.

'Is it worse than school?'

'It means Earth will no longer sustain organic life as we know it.'

'So it's not worse than school?'

Everyone on Earth should have seen it coming. Earth had been living on borrowed time for a couple of centuries already. Global warming had made life on the planet a tenuous prospect. The ice caps had long since melted and, sure enough, the seas had risen. Mining, deforestation and pollution had continued unchecked, apart from a tiny flurry of protest from the almost-forgotten 'Green' movement in the early twenty-first century. Consumers still consumed, businesses delivered like there was no tomorrow and people pretended there was nothing wrong with this. They even ignored the smell. The amount of methane gas generated by fifty billion people, two-hundred billion cattle, four-hundred-and-twenty billion sheep and the fourteen other still un-extinct species on Earth would, in itself, be enough to render most planets a little 'whiffy' to the outsider.

Regardless of what anyone thought, or argued to the contrary, the fact is: Earth stank.

It really, really ponged.

Even Hobart, clutched tightly by Gran as the family remained glued to the USI screen, could sense that something very important was happening. He stopped wagging his tail.

Hank continued. 'Scientists have been searching all the known galaxies to look for a new place for the population of Earth to live. They have located a small, pinkish planet which, after extensive, cross-cultural market research, they have decided to call . . . "New Earth" . . .'

'Pink?' said Simone, screwing up her nose.

'Meanwhile, our ever-vigilant government has been

secretly preparing for this moment. Enormous Space Arks have been built . . .'

'With taxpayers' funds, I bet,' grumbled Mark.

'All the population, all the world's art and significant architecture, and all the world's animals will be transported to this new location. Furniture, electronic equipment and personal effects are the responsibility of individual owners.'

On the screen, dramatic images of huge spaceships had appeared. They were lined up on vast launch pads, their noses pointed towards the beckoning cosmos.

'Cats will be travelling on the *Catstar*, cows will be on the *Cowstar*, dogs on the *Dogstar* . . .'

On the USI screen, the *Dogstar* appeared to be the largest Ark of them all. If sunlight could pierce the fetid cloud cover, the hull of the huge ship would gleam majestically.

A sudden thought hit Glenn and he turned to his father. 'But Dad,' he mumbled, 'if we have to go anywhere, Hobart will come with us in the *Valiant*, won't he?'

'I know what you're thinking,' said Hank on screen at that precise moment. 'Why can't our precious family pet travel with us in the comfort of our own family vehicle?'

'Exactly,' said Simone.

'Well, they can't,' snapped Hank. 'Your government has carefully planned and coordinated a complex evacuation of fifty billion people and three-thousand billion animals. For health and safety reasons, pets will travel on their own allocated vessels. It's all been arranged. Any people who can't afford their own transportation will be carried on giant space freighters like the human cattle they are. Stay tuned for non-stop coverage of the crisis. For those of you in denial, here's a baby panda . . .'

Despite the tension in the room, the image of Flopsy, a four-month-old panda chewing on a bamboo shoot at the Hong Kong Zoo, did manage to do something for Glenn. It reminded him that he was hungry.

Lincoln gently took Hobart from Gran's arms. He clutched him with uncharacteristic, open affection. For reasons he couldn't understand, he had suddenly remembered a day two years earlier – a day when Hobart had followed him to school. Lincoln's vast intellect and the fact that he was younger than everybody else in class had made him a constant target of ridicule. Lincoln's average lunchtime was spent avoiding bullies. This day, however, Hobart's presence changed everything. Lincoln was the centre of attention as fellow students fussed over Hobart.

Lincoln was liked.

Now, today, Lincoln looked down into Hobart's bright trusting eyes and sighed.

'This is very bad,' he whispered. Hobart reacted – staring back at Lincoln as if he actually understood.

There was immediate silence in the room. If Lincoln said it was very bad – well – you didn't argue with Lincoln.

Why is Lincoln hugging me? He hasn't done this for . . . months. Something just changed. They're all being extra nice to me. Okay – okay – back to the table. The

pack is very quiet. That's a bit funny. But it is manch-time so . . .

Oops . . . don't get too close to the table. Be good. Or trouble. I've got my job to do. Wait until they eat their manch. Guard the room. Then I'll have mine. That's how it is. Smallest member of the pack last.

Wait a minute. What's this? Simone's slipping me some manch! Am I imagining this? She's reaching under the table . . . She's feeding me! Just like that! Under the table so no one else can see! Wuzza!

That's a big no-no. Hobart does not get fed at the manch-table with the big ones. No way. Simone's made a mistake. Not that I'm complaining. Wait. What's that? Glenn's hand is coming down, too! More manch?? Unbelievable!

Tastes great, too! This is the best . . .

What's that? Is that . . . ? It can't be! Lincoln's hand, too? More manch? Three lots of manch under the table. Did I do something good? Something has changed.

Funny – they look a bit sad. I'll wag my wowch – that always cheers them up.

Hmmm. Nothing.

Funny . . .

Thousands of kids watched the daily preparations for the impending launch of the Space Arks from the roofs of any adjoining tall building.

The loading and fuelling of the *Catstar*, the *Horsestar*, the *Llamastar* and the *Possumstar* raced along very efficiently. The *Cowstar* was having minor issues with methane ventilation, and the *Sheepstar* was virtually ready. But it was the *Dogstar* that stood higher and prouder than the others. It positively hummed as the machines working deep within its interior did their thing. Glenn told himself those mysterious machines would be maintaining an environment perfect for the canine cargo during the *Dogstar*'s five universal-week journey to New Earth.

At each of the Space Arks, shuttle transporters were landing, depositing shipments of animals at regular intervals. Glenn could barely get his head around a tenth of the logistics needed to locate, transport and load all of the Earth's animals, and place them safely within these mighty vessels. He did, however, reflect on the fact that it was lucky there were no wild animals out there roaming willy-nilly in jungles or stalking aimlessly through forests any more. Of the sixteen species of animal that had survived mankind's unchecked greed and expansion, eight were well and truly tamed and farmed for food and clothing, five were in zoos, three were kept as pets.

And there were no forests or jungles left, anyway.

Suddenly, Glenn heard yells from the launch site. A pipe containing a greeny-blue gas had burst and come away from the ship. Glenn frowned as he watched workers hastily shut off the gas, then struggle to reconnect the pipe securely. Glenn pulled out his Planet Man figurine and whispered a question he'd been thinking about for the last twelve seconds.

'Planet Man?' said Glenn. 'You don't think anything can go wrong with the *Dogstar*, do you?'

As usual, Planet Man's eyes lit up and a pre-recorded message was forthcoming. 'In times of danger – *Glenn* – don't forget to chew Planet Man bubble gum. Now available in new, fruity kumquat flavour.'

Glenn knew that everything Planet Man said was laden with significance. Sometimes it was obvious. Sometimes it was cryptic. Glenn thought long and hard about Planet Man's words.

His eyes had begun to glaze over when the arrival of another shuttle snapped him back to reality. It was smaller than the dog transport vehicles. He watched as two robots emerged and stared up at the ship. They carried pilots' cases and Glenn registered (almost immediately) that they were the pilots of the vessel. A man in technician's overalls spoke to them. Glenn overheard.

'Crewmember designate Zeke – Crewmember designate Alice – you have your instructions. Your pre-flight programming is complete. Good luck,' said the man. He then turned and climbed back into the shuttle. It sped off.

Of course, thought Glenn. Robotic pilots. That eliminates the possibility of human error. They thought of everything.

As Glenn watched, the two robots turned towards the ramp leading to the ship's interior.

'It's a pleasure to have you assisting me on this trip, Alice,' said the first robot, striding up the ramp without looking back.

'Assisting? What do you mean, Zeke?' said the second robot, following him up the ramp.

'Just that, Alice,' said Zeke. 'I will enjoy your company as the Second Officer aboard the *Dogstar*.'

'But Zeke, there is no First Officer or Second Officer. We're equal, you and I. That much was made clear in our flight briefing.'

'Was it?'

'Yes, it was.'

'I must have missed that bit.'

At that very moment, Zeke tripped as he stepped inside the ship. He fell face first on to the hard metal floor and, with the impact, his head fell off. It bounced a couple of times making a hollow, clanging sound. It eventually came to rest at Alice's feet. If a robot could sigh, Alice would have sighed as she picked up Zeke's head and reattached it swiftly.

'Thank you, Alice,' said Zeke, getting to his feet. 'Now . . . where were we?'

Alice's reply was lost to Glenn as she led her companion into the interior of the *Dogstar*.

A small, barely perceptible feeling of unease had started to rise from somewhere near Glenn's kneecaps. It grew stronger and stronger as the day of the launch grew near. By that fateful Tuesday morning, it was positively throbbing.

Why is Simone waking me up so early?

I'm always the first one in the pack to wake up. Always. But she beat me! Now she's taking me outside! Wuzza!

This is the best! Chasing miawks. Sniffing boodahs. Sniffing poles. Sniffing no-hairs' legs. I still don't understand why the no-hairs don't join in. It's great. But Simone is thinking about something else. She keeps stopping to talk to me, saying things like 'good' and 'behave' and . . .

I think Simone looks sad.

We're back at home. What's this? Glenn needs me to take him for a walk, too?

Two walks in one day! More chasing miawks, sniffing

boodahs, sniffing poles and no-hairs' legs. How good is this? But Glenn seems a bit more quiet than normal.

Hmmm. He's stopping to talk to me, too. I don't understand what he's saying but . . . what was that word . . . 'sorry'? It might have been 'growly'. I don't know. I never really understand anything Glenn says.

Oh well, that was fun. Back at home. I think I'll have a nap. But here's Lincoln. Lincoln wants me to take him for a walk!

Three walks in one day! Wuzza! Wuzza! Wuzza! How good is that! I like this! More chasing miawks and sniffing boodahs, sniffing poles and sniffing no-hairs' legs. I've even sniffed a dead pweet, and a really pongy bit of fabulous mud! You don't get much mud in the towers. What a bonus!

But here's another funny thing. Lincoln's stopping in the middle of the walk, too. He's talking. No idea what he's saying but he looks really serious. 'Course Lincoln is always serious. He's more serious than the Doberman three doors down – what a grumpy dog. But Lincoln looks sad, too, like the others.

What's going on?

Greta Clark liked routines. She had her shopping days, her cleaning days, her self-development days. Even though her routine had been understandably interrupted by news that Earth was a doomed planet, she presided with motherly care over the family's packing for the trip to New Earth. Everyone was helping load possessions into the *Valiant*, the Clark family conveyance.

Now, the *Valiant* was not the prettiest of spaceships. It was old and rusty. Mark had picked it up cheaply several years earlier when starting up his removal business. It was slow, but relatively sturdy. Sorry – let's get real – it was a bargain. And that was its only redeeming feature.

Greta looked up as Gran, Simone and Glenn brought in a plain, brown-paper-covered shape.

She frowned.

Now, Greta is no fool and the sight of a brown-paper package shaped exactly like the family pet was justification enough for suspicion.

'Simone, you know Hobart can't come with us. He has to ride in the *Dogstar*.'

'What do you mean?' said Simone, feigning ignorance.

'You two – unwrap Hobart. You're not fooling anyone.'

'It's a vase!' said Glenn.

'Woof,' said the package.

'Shh! Bad vase!' muttered Gran.

Hobart was duly unwrapped.

In the living room, Mark sat silently. He'd landed a large moving-contract the day before. The inhabitants of Tongatapu, a Pacific island, had contracted him to move the entire contents of their island to New Earth: temples, thatched houses and the current crop of their largest export, bananas. It would be a profitable job and Mark had eagerly accepted it, but only halfway through loading the cargo he had taken time off to come home.

'Personal reasons.'

Mark sat on the sofa staring at the front door to the apartment, saying nothing.

He was waiting.

Got 'em. Careful – Mark doesn't like plurg in his slippers, so don't dribble. I'll take his slippers over and . . .

Hello? Mark? Over here.

See? Slippers?

Hmmm. Nothing.

He's not looking at me. He's just staring at the door.

Now that's just strange. More than strange.

He looks a bit worried – no, that's not it . . . it's almost like he's scared.

Poor Mark. I'll lather his hand. Might be a bit of a gamble, though. Sometimes the no-hairs get a bit testy with lathering. But I'll do anything to cheer Mark up.

Ahh! Doorbell! I get it, he was waiting for someone – visitors! I like visitors! New smells! More ruffs! Hey! What . . .?

Why is Mark picking me up? Why's he handing me to Gran? Don't I get to see the visitors? Why should Mark get all the good smells?

Plosch! Now I'm in the next room.

'I've come for the dog,' said the dog collector as Mark opened the door.

Simone, Glenn and Lincoln had rushed in quickly on hearing the doorbell. They were pressed up next to Mark. Through the open door, they could see the officer's shuttle parked on the thirty-third-floor shuttle-way.

'What dog?' replied Glenn.

The man checked his palm pilot. 'Err . . . Hobart . . . registered pet – canine – AV-90836 – domiciled at this address.'

Simone jumped in quickly. 'No. No dog here. Your

records must be out of date.'

The official smiled patiently. He lifted a small device to his mouth and blew. There was no sound, but Glenn and Simone froze when they realized it was a dog whistle.

Hobart bounded happily into the room. Gran followed him in. She shrugged to Mark, who nodded silently. The dog collector clipped a lead on to Hobart's collar and gave the family a determined look.

'He has to go on the *Dogstar* with the other dogs.'

'What's your name?' asked Simone.

'Council Ranger 9868 – Leo MacLeod.'

'Mister MacLeod . . . could you take one last photo of us together?' pleaded Simone.

Leo hesitated for a moment. He looked decidedly emotional for a dog collector. He sighed. 'Sure, sure. I know what it's like. I put my whippet on the *Dogstar* this morning. Poor little girl. She nuzzled me with her little nose, then she . . .'

'Just take the picture, please,' said Simone, handing him a camera.

Leo took the camera as the family gathered round.

'Do you know how it works?' asked Mark.

'Naturally – sorry – could you all move back a bit?'

The family took a step backwards. Simone couldn't help but notice Glenn holding up two fingers behind Hobart's head as they posed.

'Glenn, that's only funny when you do it to a person, not an animal,' said Simone.

'Oh.'

Gran muttered, 'Behave yourself, Glenn. This is all

we'll have to remember Hobart by if anything goes wrong with the *Dogstar*.'

'What!?'

'Not that it will, of course. Modern technology's marvellous.'

At that moment, Leo pushed the button on the camera. There was a burst of flame and an electric shock went right through Leo, actually rendering him transparent for the briefest of moments. Leo's high-pitched squeak sounded painful, but the family were more interested in the insta-print photo emerging from the smouldering camera now lying on the ground. It showed the Clark family surrounding Hobart.

They all looked very happy together – the perfect family portrait.

'Don't go with strangers' – that's what they're always telling me. So why are the pack telling me to go with the burnt-smelling no-hair? Who are these other dogs?

Oh . . . there's the Doberman from three doors down in the moving-thing, too. He doesn't look too happy about this. I'll ask him if . . . Okay – maybe not. He can get testy. The burnt no-hair is closing the door behind us. There're about twenty dogs in here. Mainly guys from the neighbourhood.

Aghhh! Maybe we're going to the vet!

No. No. That can't be it. My pack always comes with me to the vet. Always. It's like . . . a rule. It's not the vet. So where are we going? And why does my pack look sad?

As the door closed behind Hobart, Gran ran forward holding a small package. She pressed it into the hands of the dog collector.

'Here,' she said, 'this is Hobart's. It's a chewable toy. His favourite. Regulations say he can take one toy with him.'

'That's right,' said Leo, taking the toy and placing it in a box of similarly wrapped objects beside the driver's seat. 'I'll see he gets it.'

The shuttle started to move off. There were no emotional dramas – no tears, no shouting. Each member of the Clark family simply waved to Hobart until the shuttle was lost from sight round the corner of the building.

They stood staring for a few moments afterwards. Although they didn't say so, they were all feeling just a little more alone. And even Lincoln, who was used to feeling alone, felt more alone than he'd ever felt before.

We've stopped. Okay – that ride's over. But what's that new sound? Rumbling? It's kinda familiar but I can't quite put my paw on it. The doors are opening. Maybe I'll be able to see what it is.

Whoooooaah. The smell! So many scents! I've never smelt so many dogs together in one place! There must be hundreds! What . . .? We're going out . . .? Okay, okay, stop pushing.

Maybe now I'll see what all the fuss is ab–

Ohhhhh.

I get it. That sound. That rumbling sound. It's dogs. They're all inside that . . . thing. It's huge. It's like the Valiant but not the same brown colour. And it's bigger. It's so high I can't even see the top of it.

The smells! I'm just . . . I can't . . . It's almost hard to breathe. The smell of so many crumpers! How many of *them could possibly fit in that thing? It's almost like every dog in the world is here! And they're all talking at once.*

That's gotta be the biggest kennel in the world.

'Is that Hobart?' said Simone, pointing to the dots in the distance.

'Yes,' said Lincoln, the only one who had thought to bring binoculars along.

The Clark family were standing on a rooftop overlooking the *Dogstar*'s launch pad. Around them, a large crowd of dog-lovers, many with tears in their eyes, were watching the last of the dogs being loaded on to the spaceship.

Below the Clark family's vantage point, the final batch of around thirty dogs, having just had their health scans and final processing, were walking up the ramp into the hold on the spaceship.

'Does he look happy?' asked Glenn.

'If I were to answer "yes", it would only be a feeble attempt to bolster your spirits and I'm not normally in the habit of relaying misleading or inaccurate information.'

Glenn thought about this. 'What do you mean . . . ?'

Lincoln sighed. 'Yes – he looks happy.'

In fact, Hobart looked somewhat numb. With his senses overwhelmed by the smells and sounds of millions and millions of other dogs, he, like every other dog in the vicinity, appeared slightly disoriented. He walked up the ramp towards the entrance to 'G Hold' with Border

Collies, Basset Hounds, Scottish Terriers, Dachshunds and the Doberman from three doors down. At the top of the ramp, the tension got to him.

Let's talk for a moment about that time-honoured, canine tradition of 'marking your territory'. Don't be shy. You've seen it before. Dogs in new surroundings or territory where other dogs are present often need to mark an area to establish dominance. It's not a nasty thing. It's not an arrogant thing. It's just a dog-thing; perfectly natural. There's an old dog-saying that, loosely translated, goes something like: 'a little piddle goes a long way'.

So, as Hobart climbed the last few steps into the hold of the *Dogstar*, instinct kicked in. He couldn't help it. He lifted his leg and peed.

No one was watching, but the location of the wee was the problem. The stream landed on a hydraulic servo unit – electrically powered. There was a spark. The resultant short circuit fused wires in the local control panel. The spark then travelled through the impulse conduit line, deeper into the electronics of the ship.

As Hobart continued on into the *Dogstar*, he was blissfully ignorant of the mischievous spike of energy travelling quickly through relay wires that eventually linked into the actual launch controls of the ship.

On the bridge, robot pilots Zeke and Alice sat in their respective seats doing various routine checks. The scheduled launch time was some four hours away. Suddenly, Zeke noticed a flashing red light.

'Alice, what does it mean when that light flashes?'

'Oh – that's just the air-conditioning, Zeke.'

'Are you sure, Alice?'

'Yes, Zeke.'

'I thought it meant we're about to take off.'

'No, that can't be right. We're the pilots and neither of us has started the countdown yet.'

'Good point.'

A sudden vibration disturbed Zeke. It came from somewhere below.

'But neither of us put on the air-conditioning, either.'

Standing on the nearby roof with the rest of his family, Lincoln was the only one who noticed the sudden retraction of the ramp and closure of the door to 'G Hold'. Soon everyone realized something was up when the *Dogstar*'s engines ignited.

'Is that supposed to be happening?' asked Simone.

With a huge roar and the white-hot fury of ionized plasma engines pumping at full throttle, the *Dogstar* suddenly shot straight into the air. Well, 'straight' would be misleading. It shot up rather erratically, weaving an irregular course into what passed for the atmosphere these days. It was quickly lost amid turbulent, brown clouds.

This was all very sudden and unexpected. Everyone on the roof was silent for a few moments, then everyone started talking at once.

'That was too soon.'

'It's not supposed to leave yet.'

'What's going on?'

'Should we ask someone . . . ?'

The Clark family just stared at the hole closing over

in the depressing-looking cloud mass above them. They didn't dare ask more questions. Simone and Glenn had their fingers crossed, thinking of Hobart and hoping he was all right.

Remember that place I said we didn't want to go? Maybe not. Anyway, we're going there.

Broadly speaking, Earth cities are all the same – the higher up you live, the wealthier you are. The rarefied heights of the tallest towers hold the most privileged and important people. The air isn't any better up there, but at least you get to look down on everybody else.

As we know, the Clarks lived on the thirty-third floor of their apartment building. A fairly middle-class existence. Way, way, way down below them, however, is another world. The people at the very bottom aren't there because they've made a lifestyle choice to live simply. They're down there because there's nowhere else for them to go.

At the very bottom, where the buildings meet the surface of the planet, are the dregs of humanity. The word 'surface' is not used very much in polite society, and the term 'ground dweller' is a standard insult anywhere upwards of the fifth floor. At the bottom there's very little sunlight squeezing down between the towers. Municipal authorities don't do anything to maintain services and everything is either rusted, covered with grime, or not working properly.

That applies to the people, too.

The streets are full of rubbish – the refuse of an all-consuming society piled up in huge mounds. Since news had filtered down to the bottom about moving to a new planet, these piles had grown even larger as the people above discarded even greater numbers of unwanted items. The forgotten, miserable people who scoured these dumps to survive – the most desperate, most pathetic and most miserable human beings alive – were now finding slightly better scraps to scavenge.

At the very moment the *Dogstar* launched, two such humans were fossicking in a smelly pile of rotting food scraps. Well, the short, beady-eyed adult one was. The child was practising what looked to be a rudimentary dance step. Was it a demi plié?

'Can I show you something, Father?' said the grime-covered child.

'If it's another dance step I might have to throw this wet sock at you,' replied his father. The adult figure held up a wet sock in his hand – black in colour, with an odour best described as challenging.

'No, it's this!' replied the child.

The adult ground dweller couldn't mask his increasing irritation as the child repeated the ballet move.

'And that's not a dance step?'

'It's a defence system. Next time we're menaced by a vicious street gang, I'll do this.' The child repeated the demi plié. There was almost an element of elegance to it this time. 'They'll be so impressed, they'll run away.'

'Or they might do this!' said the adult, throwing the sock vigorously towards the child. The child nimbly ducked and the sock disappeared from view, landing with a dull thwack on something fleshy behind the rubbish pile.

'Owww,' said a voice.

Father and son were surprised when a rather shambolic figure emerged from behind the rubbish. (And remember where we are. Shambolic down here means pretty much ghastly.) The figure was an older, taller man, covered in rags and carrying a huge backpack that seemed to be crammed with objects. His eyes were wild and darted everywhere. He held the black sock in his hand.

'Who threw this sock?' he asked in a rather high-pitched whine.

'Sorry, I was aiming for my son.'

'You look kind of familiar.'

'Ever heard of Bob Santino?' said the father, more in hope than expectation. He was surprised at the response.

'The brilliant scientist?'

'You're looking at him. And one of his socks,' said Bob Santino as he took his sock back from the figure who was now twitching with nervous excitement – or fleas – perhaps both.

'But . . . but you were famous . . . what happened?'

The father, who we've now identified, took a deep breath. He looked pained. 'You'll recall I invented the famous neutron light bulb?'

'Did you?'

'Oh, yes. Sadly, the first five hundred users were turned

into ravenous, flesh-eating zombies.'

'. . . oh.'

'They brought a lawsuit against me. My company went bankrupt and now I'm reduced to living down here with the garbage.'

'He doesn't mean me,' piped up his son.

'My son, Dino. No, he's not garbage – he moves,' said Santino.

'This is an extraordinary coincidence,' said the taller man. 'I'm a scientist myself. My name is Ramon Ridley.'

'Sorry to hear it.'

'Behold my finest invention. The Robog!'

Ridley reached eagerly into his backpack and removed a set of blueprints. They depicted a dog-like, toy-like, robot-like object. The schematics were quite detailed, if a little crude.

'The Robog?' queried Santino.

'A robot dog. Rob – as in robot. Og – as in dog. Get it? Rob-og. I even built a prototype.'

Ridley reached into his backpack again and removed a small gadget. It had obviously been made from bits of junk, recycled appliances and discarded toys. He placed it on the ground, where it assumed a begging position. Its movements resembled a pitiful wind-up toy from the Victorian era. As it trundled jerkily towards him, Santino noticed that its mid-section was made from an old toaster. He jumped as a piece of toast (burnt) spat out of the dog.

Ridley beamed. 'Brilliant, wouldn't you say?'

'Not with a straight face,' said Santino.

'Sadly, I've never found anyone who was interested.'

'You still haven't.'

At that moment, there was a sudden downdraught from jet engines above them. An object was landing nearby. The gust from its landing jets blew the Robog back behind the rubbish pile. Ramon Ridley leapt after it and vanished from sight. Santino lowered a protective hand from his eyes to see a messenger-bot. The bot was a simple design – humanoid upper half and jet-thruster bottom half. Dino was impressed.

'Wow. We don't get many of those down here,' he said.

'Bob and Dino Santino? Garbage pile number 37B?' asked the messenger-bot.

'Who wants to know?' said Bob.

The messenger-bot's arm extended, handing Santino two tickets. 'Your tickets to New Earth. You're on the Space Freighter *Maximus* departing from gate lounge 7930.'

Santino frowned as he read the small print on the tickets. 'Tenth Class? There's a tenth class?'

'Enjoy your trip,' said the robot as its engines ignited and shot it into the air. Santino shook his head fatalistically.

Dino, who didn't like seeing his father depressed, tried to be cheerful.

'Cheer up, Father. Maybe things will be better on New Earth.'

'They couldn't be any worse than they are now, Dino.'

It's funny how often these innocent phrases can pre-empt events which, ironically, counterpoint them – almost as if they were foreshadowing some ghastly turn of events for comical effect.

No sooner had these words left Bob Santino's mouth

than there was a rustling behind them and then the sound of heavily booted feet crunching through rubbish. Santino and Dino turned to see five figures standing behind them. They were young, scarred from many battles and armed with pieces of metal pipe. Each of them possessed the vacant stare of the truly desensitized.

As Santino stood there, facing the five, he realized he was in trouble. Street gangs like this were merciless and desperate. Santino and Dino clearly had nothing to steal, so this particular gang just wanted to do them harm. Santino closed his eyes and waited for the inevitable. He was totally unprepared for what followed.

'Stand back!'

The voice belonged to Dino. Santino opened his eyes to find Dino had leapt between him and the gang.

'Oh no . . .' muttered Santino.

Dino immediately launched into some dramatic ballet moves. He started with a rond de jambe, moved effortlessly to a battement frappe, then a fouette, a pirouette and, finally, a fluent arabesque. It has to be said that, under pressure, Dino executed the moves with a cool precision. The gang members were frozen by the spectacle. Their leader, a weasel-featured runt, quivered.

'Run! He knows ballet!' he finally yelled, and the gang was gone in the blink of an eye. Santino looked around. He couldn't quite comprehend what had just occurred. Dino bowed elegantly.

Santino took a deep breath, then coughed as he sucked in enough toxic fumes to make an elephant dizzy. If there were any elephants any more. Which there weren't.

He took Dino's hand and started walking. 'Come on, Dino,' he said. 'It's a long walk to the *Maximus*.'

The *Maximus* was one of the last ships to depart Earth and join the vast flotilla of craft heading to New Earth. Its launch was unspectacular. Its passage to the jump-point near Jupiter was routine, apart from a near miss with a smaller, older craft that inadvertently cut across its bows while taking a last look back at its old home. That craft was the Clarks' *Valiant*.

Aboard the *Valiant*, the Clark family stared silently back at Earth with mixed feelings.

'I'm going to miss the old place,' said Mark.

'Me too,' sighed Simone.

The flotilla moved away quickly before the inevitable happened.

A series of flashes in the upper atmosphere signalled that a huge electrical storm had begun. The resultant stratospheric ionization instantly created complex chemical reactions in the soupy air. The oxygen evaporated. Methane, butane and freon fused into a brand-new element which, though scientifically fascinating, is a pain in the neck to describe accurately. Suffice to say, at one minute after three thirty p.m., there was no breathable atmosphere left on Earth.

'That's it, then,' said Lincoln, just as a proximity warning sounded and Mark made a hasty course correction that avoided collision with the fast-moving *Maximus*.

'Indicate when you change lanes!' yelled Mark.

Ahead was the jump-point. The flotilla of two million and fifty-seven-thousand spacecraft headed towards it. The huge Space Arks containing the old Earth's animals were all in the centre of the fleet. All except the *Dogstar*, which had launched earlier and had disappeared from radar screens already. As one, the swarm of private craft, industrial craft, liners, freighters and Space Arks leapt into hyperspace at the pre-programmed jump-point and vanished from the Solar System altogether.

This kennel isn't very nice. It doesn't have a smell. There're thousands and millions of dog scents everywhere. But this floor doesn't smell. It's metal. It's cold.

I can't get out. These bars of light are hot and frizzle my hair when I get too close to them. It looks like all the other dogs are in the same kind of little kennel. Through the bars of light I can see about fifty of them across the way. They're all looking out just like me. Do I look that sad, too?

There are dog voices everywhere – more dog voices

than I've ever heard before. How big is this kennel? And outside . . . that's the strangest part of all.

There's no sky out the window. How is that? Ever since I can remember, there's always the brown sky above, but outside it's black – just black with little points of light. 'Stars' Lincoln called them once when we were looking up at the sky at night. The smelly clouds had parted for once and we saw a patch of the night sky above it.

Lincoln said it was . . . 'rare'. I'm not sure what that means.

On the bridge of the *Dogstar*, Zeke and Alice stared straight ahead at the unfamiliar starfields in front of them.

'Do you have any idea where we are, Alice?' asked Zeke.

'None at all, Zeke.'

'Oh well – there's no need to worry. All the automatic systems seem to be functioning.'

'If that's true, Zeke, then why did we miss the jump-point? We haven't made the jump to hyperspace and none of these stars match records in the data banks. We're certainly not heading towards New Earth. We seem to be well off course and wandering aimlessly.'

'Well, there's no need to worry,' replied Zeke, affecting an air of confidence.

'I'm not worried, Zeke. Robots don't worry. We're incapable of worry. It's not part of our programming.'

'Really?' replied Zeke. 'How interesting. How very, very interesting. Because I'm definitely worried. I can feel it.'

'You can't be feeling anything, Zeke,' said Alice.

'And yet I am,' persisted Zeke. 'You know, Alice, I've had this feeling for quite some time now . . .'

'Being worried?'

'No. Another, stronger feeling. But being worried has only confirmed it for me. Alice – I think I'm human.'

The words just hung there for a moment. Alice shook her head, then she checked her audio-record file to make sure she'd heard correctly.

'Zeke – you can't be human. You're a robot.'

'And yet I'm not, Alice. I'm actually a human. All this time I've been quite wrong about me. Isn't that a conundrum?'

Alice was silent. Although she was only programmed for a limited range of feelings (excluding 'worry', as we've discovered), she nevertheless felt that something wasn't quite right.

I really need to go.

Really. I've been holding on since I got here, but a dog can only keep it in for so long. I had manch before I arrived at this kennel – and what goes in has to come out sooner or later. But where can I do it? There's nowhere to dig. The floor is too hard.

I'll have to do it on the floor. How embarrassing. 'Never do it inside, Hobart,' Gran says. Well – I hope none of the other dogs see me. Oh . . . here goes . . . Ahhh! That feels better.

Hmmm. What do I do with it now? It's just sitting there. Wait! What's this? What are those little things? Where did they come from? They're like shiny little toys – like Lincoln's little rocket cars – the ones he makes fly by pointing the box at them. They're scurrying around on the floor. They're cleaning up my poop! They're taking a little bit and carrying it off! How amazing! They're little cleaners!

It's almost gone! It has! It's gone. The last little toy is spraying something on the spot. It's . . . it's . . .

I can't smell a thing! The spot where I pooped doesn't have any smell at all! They've taken the scent!

I wonder where they took it? Oh well . . . Everything's back the way it was before. Maybe that's what they do. Make everything the same.

Outside the window it's still black with little stars. The window's really cold. So . . . it must be cold and empty out there.

I miss my pack. Are they somewhere in this big kennel, too? Maybe they are, but all I can hear are dogs.

My pack might be out there in the darkness? I hope they're okay without me doing stuff for them.

Some time later, in another part of the Galaxy entirely, the *Valiant* and the rest of Old Earth's spaceship fleet emerged from hyperspace. Precise targeting had brought them only a few thousand miles from a cute, pink planet bathed in the glow of a sun. It was slightly smaller than Old Earth. Ironically, because there were no rubbish dumps, nuclear-waste facilities and toxic wastelands here, there was actually more room for people. The spheroid's appearance could only be described as 'nice'.

'Nice,' said Greta as she saw New Earth for the first time.

'Nice,' agreed Gran, even though pink wasn't her favourite colour.

'Yep – it certainly is . . . nice,' said Mark as he turned the *Valiant* to the correct atmospheric entry angle.

The *Valiant* was soon hovering over a 'nice' suburb in an equally 'nice' town. Terra-forming construction teams had been busy in the last few weeks creating New Earth's new infrastructure. Prefabricated houses had been prepared, and supermarkets, shopping malls, sports stadiums and museums were ready to fill. All of Old Earth's significant architecture had been transported here and, even though some of it was still being re-erected, it created a 'homely' feel to see those familiar icons – even if the sight of the Eiffel Tower next to the Sydney Opera House was a little disconcerting at first. Similarly, the Golden Gate Bridge and the Great Pyramid of Gizeh made a rather incongruous coupling.

Still, Mark brought the *Valiant* down exactly at the address he'd been given and immediately liked what he saw.

This was their new home – a neat suburban dwelling with a lawn out front. Even though it was identical to the house beside it, and the next, and the next, the family couldn't be happier to be living in an actual suburb – not a tower. Such things were unthinkable on Old Earth, and as they stepped out of the *Valiant* into their home the Clarks felt good about their new dwelling. Only one thing was missing.

'So, when will Hobart be here?' asked Glenn almost immediately.

'Yes, where's Hobart?' echoed Simone.

'Hobart's presence would definitely enhance feelings of homeliness and togetherness,' said Lincoln.

Mark shrugged. 'I'm not sure, kids,' he said. 'I suppose it takes a few days to unload all those dogs.'

'We'll just have to be patient,' suggested Greta.

'Patience, huh!' sneered Gran. 'When you get to my age you don't have time for patience. Where's Hobart? I want to see him now.'

As the Clark family went about setting up their new house, the USI screen suddenly came alive as a priority news bulletin issued forth. As usual, a smiling Hank Henry looked unflappable as he announced the unpalatable.

'We interrupt our regular programming for a special breaking news story. The *Dogstar* has disappeared . . .'

Every member of the family stopped what they were doing and turned to the screen.

'The mighty Space Ark with all of the world's dogs has not arrived as scheduled on New Earth and long-range scans have failed to find any trace of the craft or its occupants . . .'

The Clark family were stunned and shocked. They couldn't believe what they were hearing.

'But . . . but you've been telling us everything was fine for the last five weeks!' wailed Simone to the screen.

'You will have been aware of my regular updates informing you that everything was fine with the *Dogstar*,' said Hank. 'These updates were not, strictly speaking, the truth. They were part of an elaborate cover story, created in collaboration with the best trauma counsellors and marketing experts, to minimize the panic the real story would have created. Rest assured, we did have your best interests at heart.'

Hank's calm and cheerful disposition made this all sound very right and proper.

'That makes sense,' said Mark.

Hank continued. 'But now everyone has arrived safely on New Earth, the truth can be told. And I, for one, am glad. The burden of carrying this terrible secret has weighed quite heavily on me.'

'Poor man,' said Greta.

'Exhaustive analysis of tapes from the premature launch of the *Dogstar* revealed no clues as to its disappearance. So we can only pray that it is suffering a temporary problem and that the ship will eventually find its way to New Earth, and that we will all be reunited with our beloved canine companions. Let's hope so. Because I'm really missing my little cocker spaniel, Kylie. If you're watching this, schnookums, be brave for Daddy.

'A crisis line has been set up to deal with any questions you may have. The number is on the bottom of your screen now. The relevant authorities thank you for your understanding.'

Each of the Clarks suddenly experienced a very empty feeling in their stomachs. One by one they took each other's hands. They stood silently, staring at the USI screen that now showed a story about problems encountered while reassembling the Taj Mahal. Someone had put the dome on upside down. Not one of the Clarks was listening to the story.

'But . . . Hobart,' said Glenn.

'Do you think he's all right?' asked Simone.

Lincoln was making mental calculations. 'At this point in time there has been no evidence of a catastrophic malfunction or a fatal accident. We can only hope that Hobart is safe – though missing.'

Their fear didn't abate, however. It just hung in the air, surrounding them with cold tentacles.

Each of the Clarks was thinking the same thing: 'How are we ever going to get by without him?'

The polar caps of New Earth were just as cold and inhospitable as those of Old Earth (pre global warming), and therefore, according to the thinking of planning authorities, the perfect place to house the human dregs that used to live on the lowest levels of their old planet.

Bob and Dino Santino were now shivering in their Arctic-style clothing, generously provided by the Government – paid for via low-interest loans to be repaid over ten years. They were looking across the snowfields towards a pathetic sight.

Two of their contemporaries in this miserable outpost were trying to rig up a dog sledge. In place of huskies, they'd made do with sixteen cats hitched to it.

'Mush!' yelled the driver, cracking a huge whip above them. The cats simply stood, licking themselves – the sledge didn't move a millimetre.

'Told you it wouldn't work,' said the driver's companion.

Santino smiled. Deriving humour from the misfortunes of others was one of the few pleasures left to him in this nightmarish environment.

'Father, I have an idea,' said Dino, chirpily.

It has to be said that Dino, despite his deficiencies, was always cheerful and optimistic. It would have been a very admirable trait if it wasn't so annoying.

'Shut up,' said Santino.

'It's a really good idea,' said Dino.

'Does it involve dancing?'

'It's a way to make money.'

'And not by dancing?'

'No.'

'And not through anything else involving expressive movement?'

'No.'

'No mime? No charades?'

'No.'

'All right – tell me,' sighed Santino without enthusiasm.

'You're a scientist, Father. Why don't you make these things and sell them?'

Dino pulled out a crumpled bit of paper from his pocket. It was the blueprint that Ramon Ridley had showed Santino back on Earth. The blueprint that had been sent flying from his hands by the arrival of the messenger-bot.

'I picked it up after that whiney old scientist vanished.'

Santino looked at it carefully. 'The Robog,' he muttered.

'Don't you think a robot dog would be kind of cute?' chirped Dino.

Santino looked over at the cat sledge. The driver picked up the lead cat in his harness. It was frozen solid.

Bob Santino's mind ticked over. The residents of New Earth were painfully aware that the *Dogstar* had vanished, and the wave of sadness sweeping the planet had touched all of them – even those who didn't own dogs. There was something very important missing in their new homes and everyone knew it. Looking at the Robog plans, Bob Santino suddenly realized here was a product that people would buy. And buy big!

'This might be our ticket back to the top, Dino!' cried Santino. 'I'll never tell you to shut up ever again!'

'I do have another idea – for an ice-skating show.'

'Shut up.'

In warmer latitudes, in the Clarks' new house, everything had been set up. Glenn's room had Planet Man posters all over the walls, Planet Man toys on the shelves and Planet Man comic books arranged in neat boxes with backboards and conservation-grade mylar sleeves to protect them. Simone's room had been tastefully prepared, with all her clothes arranged in alphabetical order (anoraks, beanies, cardigan, etc., etc.) and all her self-help books arranged under the Dewey decimal system. Lincoln's old room had been meticulously recreated on New Earth. His electron microscope next to his mini-cyclotron. His fusion generator opposite his artificial gravity experiment. Greta's kitchen was functioning perfectly, and Gran's room was home to her many prosthetic limbs and accessories. She was, after all, sixty-three per cent artificial. Both her legs, an arm and some of her internal organs had been updated over the years by cleverly engineered replacements. Even Lincoln upgraded one of her legs and her bionic liver.

Mark's removal business, too, had settled down to its normal routine. He'd managed to deliver the entire contents of the island chain of Tongatapu to New Earth with only a few breakages. He'd made a tidy profit but had been lumped with fifteen cases of 'bruised' bananas. The Tongatapuans had refused to take delivery of them because they believed them to be damaged in transit. Mark wasn't fussed. His insurance would cover any claims – and in any case, he loved bananas. He presented the fifteen cases to Greta enthusiastically, telling her to 'use her imagination'.

But there was no doubting the air of gloom that had settled over the new house. Without Hobart, the family felt flat. Everybody knew it. Nobody could do anything about it – though Greta tried hard.

Quite often she would catch one of the kids looking longingly at the last photo of Hobart – the one taken with the family just before his departure, the one that showed them all together, and happy.

One day, as Glenn was trying to sketch a picture of Planet Man wrestling a Space Slug, he was drawn to an advertisement on the USI screen.

'Missing your favourite pooch?' the voice-over said.

Two miserable-looking boys in a typical New Earth backyard looked up and nodded.

'Sick of throwing a stick to your cat?'

On screen, a kid threw a stick to his cat. The cat ignored it and walked away.

'Well, your prayers have been answered.'

Suddenly, happy music started and a glitzy looking Robog appeared in front of the boys. Unlike Ramon Ridley's prototype, this one was shiny, metallic and looked a bit more like a dog, without fur. The kids on the USI screen immediately hugged the Robog, which barked mechanically.

'Robogs are New Earth's favourite artificial dog! And they're fun! Buy one today or people will mock you.'

The screen showed shots of kids throwing sticks to the Robogs. Sure enough, the dogs retrieved them. There were shots of young couples walking their Robogs in the park. There were shots of old people patting Robogs as they lay on their laps.

'Robogs are the perfect companion – and an economical alternative to real friends.'

As Glenn watched, stunned, Lincoln and Simone had entered the room. They, too, were transfixed by the advertisement, which ended with a large group shot of a 'typical neighbourhood community' – multicultural, multi-income, multi-boring. They were all patting their shiny new Robogs happily as the voice-over said very, very quickly: 'Comes with a 1280-bit yapping card, tail wagging at 7000 Mhz, slobber-chip optional. Parental guidance recommended. May be harmful to children under and over ten years.'

The music ended triumphantly, but Glenn, Simone and Lincoln were unmoved. The Robog was clearly a gimmick. It lacked anything like a personality. It wasn't the sort of thing you'd rush to cuddle.

'It'll never catch on,' said Glenn confidently.

Over the next three weeks, the Robog became the highest-selling item in history. It surpassed those ancient favourites, the hula hoop, the yo-yo, the iPod and the fart colourizer, as the most popular, must-have item ever. In fact, it beat the combined sales of all these items hands down.

Bob Santino had no trouble attracting investors for his project. Within two weeks he was able to pay back his initial investment with interest. Within three weeks, with advance orders still growing, he was declared the richest man on New Earth. With a fully automatic factory in geostationary orbit above the planet, Santino was producing one Robog every three seconds. And every one of these was being bought by people desperately needing a replacement for the dogs they were missing.

In every park, kids romped with their new Robogs. In every home, Robogs fetched slippers. In front of every fireplace, Robogs slept happily. All right, sometimes a Robog chewed a paper to bits rather than retrieve it from the lawn. Sometimes an inbuilt security-system accidentally activated, and a flying Frisbee was atomized. Sometimes a Robog burying a bone dug down twenty metres or so. But in the end, it didn't matter. People bought Robogs by the truckload and generally seemed happy with them. Finally, they had a distraction. Finally, they didn't need to think about their missing dogs.

At the Clark house, however, the feelings of loss hadn't gone away. In fact, if anything, they were worse. Simone was holding the family portrait with Hobart. She stared at it longingly.

'I miss the way he used to curl up alongside me on the sofa,' she said.

'I miss the way he used to bury your hairbrush and dig it up again,' Glenn said.

'The one I use?' asked Simone.

'Yep.'

'And you never told me?'

'Nope.'

'What about germs?'

'He never seemed to mind.'

Simone's mouth was still open when Glenn noticed Hank's face on the USI screen. He turned up the volume. Hank was sitting in his interview seat opposite a short, rotund man in an expensive suit. Hank seemed to be positively gushing.

'Mister Santino,' he said, 'is it true that the success of the Robog has made you the richest man on the planet?'

To Simone and Glenn, the man opposite looked oily. The immaculate suit, manicured fingernails and multiple facials had managed to remove the dirt of the slums from the surface, but there was much deeper dirt that could never be removed from Bob Santino.

'The money isn't important, Hank,' said Santino, smiling.

'To what do you attribute the success of your invention, Mister Santino?'

'Please, Hank, call me Bob.'

'All right, Bob.'

'Actually, hearing that, I prefer Mister Santino. The fact is, Hank, that Robogs are the perfect pet. Although some people have already accused me of cashing in on the absence of the dogs on New Earth.'

'Have they? How cruel.'

'So cruel, Hank. All I was trying to do was bring a tiny ray of light into people's otherwise miserable existence. Scientific tests have shown that people who have bought my Robogs are happier, healthier and more content. Now you can't argue with that.'

'Who conducted those surveys, Mister Santino?'

'I said you can't argue with that, Hank.'

'Oh.'

'My Robogs are a success because people love them. Really love them. I take that very much to heart, Hank. By extension – I feel they're really loving me. So it's a win-win situation.'

'It certainly seems so.'

'Can I also say something even more personal, Hank?'

'Anytime.'

Santino turned to the camera. The shot switched to a close-up. Santino's cold, empty eyes tried to approximate sincerity.

'I really want to apologize to any folks out there still waiting for their Robog to be delivered. We've been inundated with orders and we're working round the clock to make sure no one goes without. If you've ordered a Robog and it hasn't arrived yet, be patient. You'll get it soon. And if you haven't ordered one . . . what are you waiting for?'

'Thank you, Bob Santino – self-made millionaire.'

'Billionaire.'

'Tell me, Mister Santino, do you think there's any hope the *Dogstar* will ever be found?'

Santino's face contorted in what seemed to be genuine anguish as he said, 'Alas, Hank, I fear the precious *Dogstar* is gone for all time. Perhaps we should all accept the fact that the robots flying that ship are hopelessly lost.'

Ironically, the broadcast was being watched by Zeke and Alice, aboard the *Dogstar*, at that very moment. Well – not exactly that very moment. There's a delay of a few universal seconds even with the most sophisticated broadcasting systems. Nevertheless, within a small window of time, Alice reacted to Santino's assessment.

'Hey, Zeke!' said Alice. 'He's talking about us!'

'Alice, that broadcast is coming from New Earth.'

'So?'

'Well, all we have to do is triangulate the source of the transmissions, then we'll lock in the coordinates and we'll be back on course!'

'And do you know how to do that?'

There was a pause as Zeke sighed. 'No, Alice. I don't.'

'Well, it's silly to suggest something you can't do.'

'I'm sorry, Alice. I'm only human. And it's human to hope.'

'You're not human.'

'Am so.'

With that, Zeke reached across to a master control switch. He flicked it up and down. As he did so, all of the ship's lights went off – then on – then off – then on.

Alice was bewildered. 'What are you doing now?' she asked.

'Communicating with flashing lights. It's an Old Earth technique.'

'Your logic parameters are scrambled to an unprecedented degree.'

'Not so, Alice. The data banks tell me that old-time sailing ships used this method. Maybe it'll work for us.'

Alice became aware of a howling noise coming from the bowels of the ship. The dogs were getting upset by the flashing lights.

'And who do you expect will see this?'

'Anyone passing by, Alice!' said Zeke, flabbergasted that she couldn't see the cleverness of his plan.

'It's annoying the dogs!' yelled Alice, exasperated.

'How can you tell?'

Alice didn't reply. In that moment, Zeke finally heard the clamour the dogs were making.

'Is that the dogs? I thought the turbo thrusters needed servicing.'

This isn't good. My pack must be really missing me, now. They need me. Otherwise Mark has to find his own slippers and the young ones don't have anyone to take them on walks. Who is going to bring back the ball Simone likes to throw? Who is going to protect them?

What's this? The door above me is opening again. Why? I just ate. It's too soon for manch. Wait – what's that?

Hey! It's my toy. My chewy toy fell out of the door! Didn't Gran give it to the burnt-smelling man? But how did it . . . ? Who cares! This is great! Something to chew!

Yummmmm! I love this toy! When Simone throws it, I catch it. You can chew and chew it, and it never breaks! I chew as hard as I can and it's always good to go! I've had it forever. I can throw it myself, too! Wow! Look at it go! It bounces off the walls just like it's always done. I love this! There it goes! Yesss! Caught it! I'll throw it again! Yess!

No! Arrgghhh! It's gone through the bars of light! Wait. It bounced off the wall and it's coming back to . . . Oh, no. The bars of light have gone. Did I do something wrong? Am I going to get into trouble? I can't see anyone coming. Maybe I'd better get my toy and hide it. Here it is. Got it.

Wasn't me. I didn't do it.

Feels good to be out in the big kennel. There's room to run out here! Wuzza!

Hmmm, all the other dogs are looking at me. They've all gone quiet.

Wow . . . I can see further, now. There are dogs everywhere! The little kennels with the bars of light go way into the distance. And above me, too! Look at all the dogs up there! They're all looking at me.

I don't think I'll go back into my kennel just yet. Come on, toy, let's have a look around.

'Kids, have I got a surprise for you!' Mark announced as he entered the front door.

'What is it?' asked Glenn.

Mark stepped aside in the doorway. Behind him stood a ghastly apparition. It was a brand-new Robog. Its burnished grey exterior glinted soullessly in the light. The kids looked horrified.

'It's a Robog!' said Mark, triumphantly. 'The new Series VII with Walkies plug-in!'

'But we don't want a Robog,' said Glenn, firmly.

'We want Hobart,' said Lincoln.

Mark put a fatherly hand on Lincoln's shoulder. 'I miss Hobart as much as you do, kids. But this is the next best thing. Come on, I want to see you smile again. Isn't he . . . or she . . . er, it . . . cute?'

As Mark spoke, the Robog did its best to live up to expectations and assumed a sit-up-and-beg position. If it wasn't so transparently lifeless and mechanical, you could almost feel something for it. The kids weren't easily taken in, however. But they didn't want Mark to feel bad, either.

'Yeah. Thanks, Dad,' said Simone.

'Watch him. He moves just like a real dog,' said Mark, trying to get the kids involved.

The Robog started sniffing around its new territory. The micro-processors in its electronic brain were in object-recognition mode, memorizing and categorizing each new thing it saw. Glenn, Simone and Lincoln were recognized and categorized as 'clients'. The furniture was recognized as 'disposable'. The floor covering it read as 'cheap'. Then it came across the photo of Hobart and the family. It stared at it for a moment, then, somewhere in its brain, an electronic synapse collapsed. A momentary glitch in its software resulted in a categorization of 'stick'.

The Robog immediately grabbed the photo in its jaws.

'Arrgghhhhh!' was the simultaneous yell from Simone, Glenn and Lincoln. As one, they threw themselves on to the Robog and grappled for the photo.

Mark was shocked.

'Kids, be careful with the new . . .'

But the kids weren't stopping. The Robog growled electronically and held on to its 'stick'. Simone had both hands on the photo, pulling. Lincoln was trying to pry the Robog's jaws open. Glenn yanked at its hind legs. With a huge effort, the photo was wrenched free. At the same time the Robog's head flew off and its hind legs were torn away. The rest of its body rebounded off the nearest wall and shattered into pieces. The kids didn't notice. They only had eyes for the treasured photograph.

'It's okay! The picture is okay!' cried Simone.

'Phew!' said Glenn.

'Thank goodness,' sighed Lincoln.

Mark looked at the pieces of shattered Robog lying around. He was just wondering how he'd explain this on a warranty claim form when, suddenly, the pieces started to move!

Drawn towards each other by magnetic attraction, each individual part of the Robog swirled back to a central point. Wiring reconnected, joints reattached, couplings recoupled. After twenty seconds, the Robog was reassembled.

It barked its strange, electronic squawk.

Simone, Glenn, Lincoln, and even Mark, looked on and could say nothing. There was something very disturbing about this undying, immortal monster.

'We've really got to find Hobart,' said Simone.

'I agree,' said Glenn.

'But how?' sighed Lincoln. 'That's the question.'

On New Earth, life was good. Jetestrians zipped through the air with their jetpacks, hover-cars zoomed past in their allotted airspace, people everywhere bustled around just as they had done on Old Earth.

There were subtle differences here, of course. Some people, like Mark Clark, could mow their lawns. Lawns weren't rare museum-pieces here – the sun actually shone brightly enough to promote growth of grass and the rain wasn't predominantly acid.

You could swim in all kinds of water – sea water, river water, lake water. It wasn't closed off with signs warning the unwary about toxic algae-bloom, and it didn't even have a crust.

Most of all, you could walk. Especially in parks – parks with trees, parks with flowers, parks with budgerigars (the one species of bird remaining).

In the centres of the cities, things were starting to look like Old Earth, however. Already, buildings were tall, commerce was bustling, and electronic billboards sold you everything you didn't think you needed.

Some billboards screened the SRC (Santino Robotics

Corporation) logo, which shone brightly. Bob Santino's face appeared to make another live midday appearance in what was rapidly turning into a regular slot.

'Hello, friends, I'm Bob Santino,' he said smoothly.

Let's give credit where credit's due – Santino's image had improved markedly since we first met him in the rubbish on Old Earth. The general population had a positive feeling about him. Some even looked forward to his regular broadcasts.

There were moments, however, when Santino made his fans feel uneasy. Particularly when he smiled.

He was smiling broadly right now.

'You know what's more important to me than my billion-dollar Robog business? I'll tell you truthfully – I'm being quite candid here – it's the return of the *Dogstar*.'

'Nice guy,' said a passerby, looking up at the screen. He was obviously a nitwit or an employee of SRC.

'And so I've decided to fund a brand-new school for the highly intelligent, and the just plain nerdy, to solve our problem of finding the *Dogstar*. With my money, and the brightest young brains on New Earth working on the problem, it should only be a matter of time before we find our missing pets. Let's bring those doggies home!'

There was scattered applause in the streets. For a few minutes at least, people started smiling genuinely. Hope had been kindled.

At the Clark house, Simone was berating Glenn.

'I've told you not to come into my room without buzzing!' she shrieked.

'What's the big deal?' sneered Glenn, as he peeled another Tongan banana. 'There's nothing here I'm interested in. Your life is boring, Simone. No one wants to spy on you if that's what you're thinking!'

'Then why are you here?'

'I think we should borrow the *Valiant* and look for Hobart,' said Glenn decisively.

Simone tried to speak but couldn't. So radical, so outrageous and so decisive was Glenn's suggestion, that it staggered her.

'We – we can't do that,' she said, eventually.

'Why not? We've got to do something. I miss Hobart. I want him back.'

'So do I – but we're kids. Dad isn't going to lend us the *Valiant*. Besides, I'm sure other more qualified people are looking for . . .'

'No, they're not. No one's doing anything. They're just waiting! Well, I'm sick of waiting!' said Glenn, even more decisively. 'Planet Man wouldn't wait!'

The words hit a soft spot in Simone. For some reason, she remembered an incident with Hobart six months earlier. Returning home from the park with him, Simone had been halted by three girls standing in the access to level thirty-three. These girls were the 'butch-tanks' from school.

And they didn't like Simone.

They didn't say anything. They just stood there. Simone knew there would be trouble if she tried to walk past them, but she also knew there would be a half-hour walk to the next access point. So she stood there, stewing – procrastinating – trying to decide what to do.

She wasn't prepared for Hobart charging the girls and barking at them. Naturally, the girls ran off screaming. Hobart was able to sense exactly what was required in the situation. Simone wished she had that instinct, and she didn't like Glenn reminding her of this.

'You can't live life according to what your toy tells you!'

'It's not a toy, Simone!'

'Is!'

'Isn't!'

'Is!'

'Isn't!'

At that moment, Lincoln entered the room.

'Don't you get tired of endless sibling in-fighting?' he asked. 'It's unproductive and demeaning.'

Simone and Glenn thought about this.

'No,' they answered, almost in unison.

'Well, please desist while I replay you something you may find informative.'

Glenn and Simone watched as Lincoln replayed the Santino broadcast on his communicator. The hologram of Santino, hovering above Lincoln's wrist, made them uneasy. After the message, Lincoln turned off the image.

'So?' said Glenn.

'Isn't it obvious? I've applied online already to this school. Supported by Bob Santino's limitless funds, I'm sure I can invent a Dogstar detection device very quickly.'

Glenn placed a hand on Lincoln's shoulder. He tried to let him down gently.

'Lincoln, they'll be getting applications from all over New Earth. The smartest kids in all the world will be going there. What are the chances you'll get in?'

'I've already been accepted,' announced Lincoln. 'Apparently, my scholastic achievements and IQ score are the highest ever measured for a five year old.'

'But . . . but . . . did you get Mum and Dad's permission?' asked Simone.

'No.'

'Did you talk to Gran about this?'

'No.'

'But . . . but . . . you can't just run off like this, Lincoln,' lamented Simone. 'It's . . . it's . . .'

'Well, at least he's doing something, Simone,' said Glenn. He turned to Lincoln. 'Well done, Lincoln. Great idea. I think I'll apply to go to this school, too.'

'That would be futile,' Lincoln replied.

Glenn had no idea what the word 'futile' meant, but he quickly sent through his school marks and IQ score to Santino's School for the Gifted. It took all of three seconds for his online application to be rejected.

'I wonder why they didn't choose me?' wondered Glenn out loud.

'Probably for the same reason they didn't choose that banana,' sighed Simone.

Regardless of Simone's fears, Mark, Greta and Gran were delighted when they heard Lincoln had been accepted into Bob Santino's prestigious educational facility.

'You've made us so proud, Lincoln,' said Mark. 'I always said you took after me. Remember my report cards, Mum?'

'I never saw them,' said Gran. 'You used to eat them.'

I'm hungry. How long have I been walking? Is it more than a day? The lights go on for about a day. Then off for about a night. They've already turned off once, but now they're on again . . . so it must be a new day. I think. These corridors go on forever. And they all look the same. I think I'm lost.

I'm sure it's past my manch-time. I see manch dropping into other dogs' bowls but they're not going to share it with me. They don't know me – or my crumper – or my wowch. Why would they share?

When you meet a new dog, you're supposed to sniff each other's crumpers. And wag your wowch. That's how it works. That's how you get to know each other. If you talk without doing that . . . well . . . it's rude!

Where's my little kennel? I thought I would've found it again by now.

At least I've still got my toy. Pity I can't eat it.

What's that? It's those little cleaner-toys. What are they doing? Oh . . . right . . . they're cleaning up that kennel over there. They're so fast – like lots of mice – but harder.

Where are they taking that dog's poop? Maybe I'll follow them.

They're like a pack, too. They stick together. They work together. So maybe they eat together. Maybe they've got manch.

Don't let them see you. Be careful. You don't know these guys. Sometimes new packs aren't so friendly. Hey – there's a door. They're all coming and going through it. Maybe that's where they take all the . . .

Wheeww! That smell! That's where they take all the poop, that's for sure. All sorts. German Shepherd poop. Beagle poop. St Bernard poop. Smells like it's all in there.

It looks like the little guys have finished. They're moving off. Okay, I'm curious. I need to see this. Where is all this poop? Let's see . . .

Oh . . . I thought it would be more exciting. Just a big, round box full of poop. On the other side of it there's another door leading to the black sky outside. I wonder what happens when the poop box is full? Maybe I'd better leave before the little guys come . . .

Aghhh! It nearly got me! The inside door's slammed shut! Bang! I nearly had my wowch in there! I could've been squished! Lucky I got out in time.

Oh no! My toy! It's stuck. Pull! Pull! It won't budge! If those cleaner-toys come back, they'll take it! They'll see it and grab it! I can't let that happen!

But if I stay here, they'll grab me, too.

Santino's School for the Gifted loomed large as the Clark family's air-car pulled to a stop. Santino had spared no expense on the facility. He'd briefly negotiated to buy the Leaning Tower of Pisa – he'd even offered to straighten it – but Italian authorities were reluctant to part with the item. Instead, Santino had designed something even grander and stuck his name on it.

As Mark stared up at the building he couldn't help but feel small. It didn't stop him from talking, however. 'I wonder where you get your brains from, Lincoln?' he mused as Lincoln climbed out beside him.

'There are some questions even the greatest intellects can't answer,' was the reply.

'If you say so, Linc.'

At that moment, a shiny black jet-limo screeched to a halt in front of them. Mark was surprised and delighted as a door hissed open and Bob Santino (looking shorter than on the USI screen) stepped out. Mark's hand shot out. 'Uhhh . . . Mister Santino? Robog inventor? It's a real pleasure to . . .'

Mark's words were abruptly cut off by the dramatic arrival of a figure who grabbed Mark's wrist and, crouched in a ninja fighting pose, looked ready to render Mark powerless. Mark couldn't have known that Santino, who was becoming more security-conscious every day, had recently hired a rather lethal female bodyguard. This protector, named Daina, was now only seconds away from breaking some vital part of Mark's body.

'Prepare to be neutralized,' she cried.

'Ahhh!' said Mark, his standard reply in this type of situation.

'Stand down, Daina!' shouted Santino as he stepped forward. 'We don't need any more lawsuits today.'

Daina immediately released Mark.

Santino smiled politely. 'Sorry, my bodyguard is a tad over-eager. If you want an autograph, just send in a written request and payment of the mandatory fee.'

'Mister Santino. This is my father,' said a voice.

Santino turned to see Lincoln on the steps of the school. His jaw dropped.

'Adopted?' he asked.

'No.'

'Well – I'm delighted to meet you . . . um . . .'

'Mark. Mark Clark.'

'Terrific. Lincoln is going to be my star pupil.'

'What about me, Dad?' came a voice.

Dino was climbing out of the jet-limo. Like Santino, he'd undergone quite a make-over since the last time we saw him. He was dressed in natty shorts and a well-cut school blazer. He wore a cute school cap on his head with the SRC logo deftly hand-embroidered on it.

'And you'll be a star too, Dino,' said Santino. He muttered to Mark. 'Kids, eh? You gotta love 'em.'

Santino placed his arm on Lincoln's shoulder.

'Come along, Lincoln – let's get that prodigious brain of yours harnessed.'

'Mine too, Dad?'

'You read my mind, Dino.'

Santino led Lincoln towards the doors with Dino and Daina following closely. As Mark took a step in their direction, two snarling Guard-Robogs, black in colour and dribbling artificial saliva, leapt at him. It was only titanium chains that held them in check, inches from Mark's throat.

Santino turned, irritated by the noise. 'Um . . . sorry, what was your name again?' he asked.

'Mark. Mark Clark . . .'

'Sorry, Mark. No unauthorized persons beyond this point. You understand.'

'But Mister Santino,' asked Lincoln, 'perhaps my father might like to see where I study?'

'Not possible. Rules are rules.'

Lincoln felt uneasy as the doors closed behind Santino, Lincoln, Dino and Daina. Mark stared in after them.

'Bye then, Linc . . .'

Being the start of a new week, the school's auditorium was full. It was Bob Santino's practice to start Mondays with an address to the assembled body of gifted students. It was his way of motivating them. The brightest young minds on the planet, New Earth, stared up at the short, stocky man on the podium. And they listened. Almost respectfully.

'Students – as you know, this school exists for one purpose.'

'Movement work?' asked Dino, sitting in a chair beside the podium for reasons known only to Dino. Santino hesitated.

'Okay – two purposes.'

'Voice work?'

'Okay – okay – this school has several functions, but the primary one is to find our beloved, missing Dogstar.'

In the audience, Lincoln nodded.

'Those poor, lost, lonely canines need their homes. And this institute, funded by my own sweat, exists primarily to return those missing doggies – nay, members of the family – safely back to New Earth.' Santino paused briefly. 'Amen.'

There was a burst of warm applause from the floor.

'Your efforts to develop a long-range Dogstar detection system are coming along beautifully. Keep up the good work. Remember, Bob Santino spares no expense for excellence! Good luck!'

The applause was even bigger this time.

'I have a question,' came a voice from the floor.

Santino was surprised. The speaker was Lincoln. 'Why do you require us to sign contracts granting all legal rights in whatever we create here to you?'

Santino flinched for just a split second. Then that oily smile returned.

'It seems only fair, Lincoln. After all, I'm providing you

with a nurturing environment, a warm and fuzzy support infrastructure. And the Santino Robotics Corporation is better placed to develop your ideas than you are. After all, you're children. Right?'

Though Lincoln was silent, around him there was even louder applause. So loud that no one heard Santino whisper to Daina who stood behind him. 'Intelligent sheep – quite a novelty.'

Everyone filed into the main engine room of the school – the laboratory. It provided the students with whatever they required to build anything they could imagine. And these students could imagine quite a bit.

In individual cubicles, unique dog-detecting inventions were being created.

For example, in cubicle twenty-four, someone had conceived a highly sensitive listening device – much like a very powerful radar gun. A short distance away was a digital recorder. A fellow student pushed 'play' on the recorder and the faintest sound of a dog barking was replayed back. The sound was instantly amplified by the detector with such force that the student who was holding it had all his clothes blown off. This was not the intended function of the device.

'Needs adjustment,' the student noted coolly.

In cubicle thirty-three, a different dog detector was being manufactured. It resembled a large bazooka but was, in fact, an intense energy emitter that could detect dogs hidden behind any object. The student placed a toy dog in a cardboard box and then turned the device on it. Like an X-ray, the particle beam penetrated the box, rendering it transparent. The shape of the dog could be seen inside.

But a power surge heated the target, setting the box alight and leaving the toy dog a smouldering ruin.

'Needs adjustment,' said this student.

In cubicle forty-nine, the student within was experimenting with a hovering, satellite-like device that, when it detected a dog-like shape, would instantly pinpoint it with a laser-like beam. The problem was that when the beam hit the cut-out picture of the dog the student held up on a stick, the satellite charged straight at it! It hit the cut-out and kept going, smashing into the wall and embedding itself there.

'Needs adjustment,' the student observed.

Lincoln's cubicle was number seventeen. Other students tended to stay away from this one. Strange sounds and lights would come from inside it and Lincoln himself could be a fairly intimidating figure for a five year old. He tended to work alone and seemed uninterested in fraternizing with the other students.

The one person who had no problems whatsoever with entering Lincoln's cubicle was Dino. Perhaps he was too unsophisticated to recognize genius at work – perhaps he was just too self-absorbed to react to the 'stay away' aura Lincoln exuded. Perhaps he was just thick.

Whatever the reason, Dino made a habit of dropping into Lincoln's cubicle whenever he felt the need for a chat. Lincoln usually did his level best to ignore him.

'I don't think my father understands me,' said Dino one day.

'That's normal,' replied Lincoln.

'What are you doing?' Dino asked, as if noticing for the

first time that Lincoln's work involved a rather peculiar object.

In a glass cage on his desk, Lincoln was working on something pink and fluffy, prodding it with mechanical arms. The object seemed pin-cushioned, with wires and electrodes sticking out of it at every angle. It wasn't the first time that Dino had seen this peculiar experiment, but it was the first time that he'd seen it stand up on four legs and stretch.

'This is a genetically modified super-cat,' Lincoln explained patiently. He examined a read-out he was getting on a nearby screen. He seemed happy with the figures. The cat was average-sized and pink – pink nose, pink eyes, pink fur. It seemed more interested in sleeping than anything else.

Dino watched numbly. After a while, he asked again: 'Like I said, what are you doing?'

'I'm enhancing the cat's natural odour-detecting abilities far beyond your tepid ability to comprehend. This cat's nose can now detect a single dog hair from a distance of five light-years.'

'It's a nice pink,' observed Dino.

'A by-product of the genetic engineering.'

'I'm doing a painting . . .'

Lincoln was so taken aback by this simple statement that, for the first time in days, he turned towards Dino. Dino's cubicle was right next door to Lincoln's. On an easel inside it, a portrait was visible. It was a hand-painted study of Bob Santino, in oils. It was amateurish, but recognizable.

'What is its function?' asked Lincoln.

'It's a "welcome home" present. For the dogs when they return.'

At that moment a buzzer sounded. Lincoln turned back to his own experiment. On his monitors, graphs were peaking, lights were turning green and readings were positive. Lincoln smiled a thin, satisfied smile.

'At last. Finished. Everything works. Everything is flawless.'

He removed the wires and electrodes from the large, pink feline then took it from the glass cage. It seemed to enjoy lounging limply in his arms and looked around the room as if it owned it.

'Except – you need a name. I think I'll call you . . .'

'Barbara?' suggested Dino.

'Boombah!' cried Lincoln. The cat didn't react.

'Would you call that a "pink-pink" or a "mushroom-pink"?' asked Dino, just as an announcement came over the PA system.

'Could Lincoln Clark report to Mister Santino's office immediately, please?'

Lincoln frowned.

'I see my favourite student hasn't signed his contract yet,' said Santino as Lincoln sat in a chair in front of his massive desk.

'That's correct. I haven't.'

'Why is that, Lincoln?'

'I'm uncomfortable with the thought of anyone getting all the profits from my creativity,' said Lincoln evenly.

'Are you saying you don't trust me, Lincoln?' said

Santino, doing a reasonable impression of a caring person.

'Not at all,' replied Lincoln. 'I simply want to discuss the matter with my parents before signing any legal documents. That's appropriate, isn't it?'

Santino gritted his teeth. He couldn't very well argue with Lincoln's logic.

'Of course, Lincoln. Discuss away. I welcome that. Bob Santino is nothing if not understanding. You may go.'

He ushered Lincoln out with a wave of his hand as Dino entered the room through another door.

'Would you like to hear the tune I just composed, Father?' asked Dino.

'Later, Dino,' replied Santino testily. 'I'm busy trying to find the *Dogstar*, remember?'

'Ohhh. Right. Can I ask a question, Father?'

'If you must.'

'I don't quite understand. If you find these dogs and bring them back to New Earth, won't that mean that people won't want your fabulous Robogs any more?'

'You think so, Dino? You really think so?'

Outside the door to Santino's office, Lincoln had hesitated. He'd slipped his foot inside so that the sliding door was open a few universal inches. He couldn't help but listen in as Dino spoke.

'Yes. It will definitely be bad for business. Of course, if you listened to me and marketed more pastel-shade varieties . . .'

'Listen, Dino,' hissed Santino. 'I'm not interested in bringing these rabid mongrels back to New Earth! Do you think I'm stupid? When I find the *Dogstar*, I'm going to destroy every last one of those dogs! It's insurance, Dino. No more mangy mutts! Only Robogs!'

Lincoln removed his foot and the door closed noiselessly. His blood had just run very cold.

Pull! Pull!

My toy's still stuck. But I'm not going to leave it, no matter what. My pack would never leave me, would they? So I'm not leaving my toy.

Was that a noise? Was it the cleaner-toys? Are they here? I'll stand still – show them I'm not scared.

They're not moving, either. Except . . . more of them are coming.

And more.

And more.

If I run, maybe they'll follow me. Maybe they'll leave my toy alone. Run! Run! Good – they're chasing. They must think I'm dirt that has to be cleaned up. Run!

Don't let them get close. Come on! You're faster than

them. Look behind . . . how many . . . Whoa! There're hundreds of them, now! I can only just stay ahead of them. The dogs are barking.

When I get round this corner I'll . . . Oh no! More of them coming round the corner! This way! No – this way!

Faster! Faster! They know this kennel way better than I do. How can I surprise them? How can I trick them to . . .

That smell! I've gone in a circle! I'm back at the door that grabbed my toy! And it's open! The cleaner-toys have got my toy. They're taking it inside. No way! I'm bigger than them! I'll get it!

Got it! Oh! Cleaner-toys are still holding on to it. Shake them! Ha! They're flying everywhere! Now run! Run!

Over there. There's a little door. I hope it's a door. Yes. It's all flappy. It's like a doggy door. I can just squeeze through.

Oops. Maybe I can't! I'm stuck! Halfway through! I can hear those little scuttling feet getting closer! Come on, Hobart! Squeeze! Squeeze! Breathe in! Ahhh! I'm through!

Keep moving. They're too close now to . . . Wait. The scuttling noise has stopped. They're not following me through here. Why not? Are they scared of all the wires and pipes in here? Wires and pipes don't hurt unless you fang into them. I know that much.

Maybe it's not their territory?

I'll creep back and see what's happened. Careful . . . Careful . . . Hmmm. There they are – hanging around outside the little door. They're cleaning again. What are they cleaning this time?

Oh . . . I get it. I must have left some hairs when I squeezed through. They're picking them up. They're fussy. They seem happy . . . now they've picked them all up. The little sprayer toy is spraying the anti-smell stuff. It's all clean again. Now they're moving away.

Maybe it's not their job to clean in this little corridor. Maybe this isn't their territory.

I'll keep going this way then. My pack might be somewhere else in this big kennel.

If they are, I'll find them.

At the Clark residence, Glenn and Simone were still arguing over the merits of taking the *Valiant* to look for the missing *Dogstar*. Well – Simone was. Glenn was busily watching an episode of *Planet Man*.

'We can't just take it,' Simone complained. 'Dad

wouldn't have anything to move things with. He runs a removal business, Glenn! What's he supposed to do? Carry things on his back?'

'Think about it, Simone. We wouldn't be gone very long. Fortune favours the brave, right, Planet Man?'

As usual, Planet Man's eyes lit up as it answered. 'Nobody – *Glenn* – can stand up to a real hero.'

'You're completely deluded,' Simone said.

'Well, at least I'm not a girl!' came Glenn's snappy retort.

On screen, Planet Man was confronting a den of villainous alien racketeers. (And I should point out here, we're talking about the live-action episodes – the series starring Bud Rafferty, not the later, inferior, animated series.)

As the inevitable fighting began, Simone shook her head. 'How could we possibly pilot the *Valiant* across billions of miles of space without getting lost?' she asked sensibly. 'Lincoln is the only one who knows about navigation. It would be impossible to attempt anything like this without Lincoln's help.'

At that moment, Lincoln, having left school early, came rushing in.

'Listen, both of you,' he said. 'We need to take the *Valiant* immediately and find the *Dogstar*!'

'That's what I've been saying!' shouted Glenn. 'You mean, you'll join us?'

'Yes,' said Lincoln. 'But we must leave tonight.'

'Yessss!' cried Glenn, happily. 'Hear that, Simone? Lincoln's coming. Got any more reasons to stall?'

Simone shrugged. 'No,' she sighed.

At that exact moment on screen, another alien scumbag fell, tentacles twitching. Planet Man was now repeatedly beating another alien with a steel girder and shouting, 'No one can stand up to a real hero.'

'Excellent. We leave tonight,' said Lincoln. 'Now I only need help with one little favour before we go.'

Glenn and Simone were silent. This was a rare moment in time. Lincoln had never asked them for help with anything before.

Ever.

Three hours later, it was dark. Lincoln, Glenn and Simone were in the bushes near the statue of Bob Santino, just outside Santino's School for the Gifted. Simone was very worried now. Glenn was just confused. They were both dressed in black and starting to wonder why.

'The target is inside,' whispered Lincoln. 'Follow me.'

'Target?' said Glenn. He was still bewildered by the turn of events. He dimly understood that Lincoln had agreed to join the search for the *Dogstar* – that was good. But what were they doing here? What was going on?

Lincoln crawled to the side of the building.

'There's no way we can get in, Lincoln,' said Simone. 'They've got Guard-Robogs, state-of-the-art security.'

Lincoln held a finger to his lips. He took a small device from his pocket. It was an unremarkable-looking object with a couple of switches and lights on it. Lincoln pressed a switch. A dull hum, slowly growing in pitch, came from the box. Just as it hit a certain high note, a light on it glowed green and a window above them opened. Lincoln nodded.

'Come on,' he said.

Quickly, Lincoln, Simone, then Glenn scrambled in.

'I hope you know what you're doing,' said Simone as Lincoln lowered the window.

Just before it was fully closed, however, Lincoln heard a sound. Something was approaching.

The children ducked low as a jet-limo pulled up outside the main entrance. Santino emerged, dragging Dino with him. He didn't look happy.

'A pink cat?' Santino scowled. 'A cat that can smell dogs from five light-years away? Why didn't you tell me about this before, Dino?'

'I didn't think it was important.'

'Tell me everything right now!'

'Well – I was telling Lincoln how you didn't understand me. He seemed to empathize at first . . .'

'Not that! Tell me about the cat!'

'Can I mime it?'

'No!'

'Can I draw it?'

'I'm losing patience, Dino. The cat!'

'But I didn't think you'd be interested in it.'

'Of course I'm interested. This pseudo-cat detects dogs!'

Santino finally lined up his left eye correctly with the iris scanner and the door opened. He dragged Dino inside the school. The door slammed behind them.

Lincoln closed the window, then strode purposefully off towards the laboratory. Watching him disappear into the darkness, Glenn and Simone knew they had no choice but to follow.

•

On the bridge of the *Dogstar*, Zeke was thinking. Well, actually he was processing sequences of random associations. While Alice scanned through databanks of star charts, fruitlessly looking for recognizable galaxies, Zeke moved once more towards the food synthesizer. He was a robot on a mission.

After a few moments, Alice noticed Zeke was not in his customary position. Looking around, she was surprised to see Zeke filling up a large bag with dog biscuits that were pouring from the synthesizer.

'Zeke?'

'Yes, Alice?'

'Have you had another idea?'

'Yes, Alice.'

'I thought so,' Alice sighed. 'Am I going to regret asking what it is you are doing?'

Zeke had to think about this. 'Quite possibly, Alice,' he replied. He walked off carrying the large bag. It was filled to the brim.

I've lost count of how many levels I've come down. On every level there are more dogs – more dogs than I ever imagined. But no sign of my pack.

Oops. Dropped my toy. Come here, toy. I'm not letting you go. You're the only thing I've got to remember my pack. If you forget your pack, you're lost. I'm not going to do that.

No way. Mark, Greta, Gran, Simone, Glenn and Lincoln. Mark, Greta, Gran, Simone, Glenn and Lincoln . . .

There's more black out this window, too – with the 'stars'.

Wait . . . What's that? Floating by the window – it's manch! It's the manch-biscuit-things that Gran always brings me! Why are they floating out there? Where are they coming from? Are they coming from inside the big kennel?

I can hear voices. Maybe it's the cleaner-toys . . . no . . . they don't speak. I'll see if I can get closer. But not too close. Be careful, Hobart . . .

There's something funny. At that chute. Two . . . what are they? They're like that thing Glenn carries around, but bigger. Big dolls. The louder one's pouring a bag of the manch-biscuits into the chute. The other big-doll is arguing with him. 'Stupid!' she's saying. I think I know what that means. Mark says it when he's angry with me sometimes.

The one with the bag has mentioned 'a trail'. Is that like when you leave a scent for someone to follow? Is that what the loud big-doll is doing? The other one doesn't look too happy about it. I don't blame her. I'd rather eat that manch than throw it away on a trail like that.

The loud one has closed the chute, now. He's grabbed the bag and is walking off. The other one is leaving, too. Is that . . .?

Yessss. They're leaving the trail on this floor! There are bits of manch-biscuit on the floor! All for me! No . . . wait. What about the cleaner-toys? They think it's dirt. They'll be coming to clean it up soon.

I have to grab it before the cleaner-toys do. Have the big dolls gone? I hope so. Go!

Yummm. Good stuff. But it's not enough. A pity there isn't any more.

Quick! Quick! Get back inside the little corridor before the other cleaner-toys come.

Yes. There they are. They can't see me here. They're looking around. About twenty of them are cleaning up some crumbs that were too small for me to lick. The others are wondering what happened to the rest of it! Wuzza! Yes! Beat them!

Keep going down. I'll stick to this little corridor for a while – till I'm well away from those cleaner-toys. I'll just follow my nose.

In here I'll be safe until I find my pack.

Lincoln guided Simone and Glenn through the maze of corridors towards 'the target'. Guard-Robogs frequently prowled the corridors. If Lincoln detected their presence nearby, he'd instruct Simone and Glenn to stand perfectly still. The Robogs had movement sensors that were fairly easy to get around if you were patient. The children made their way as quickly as possible deeper into the building. They needed to get to Boombah before Santino did.

Another clever electronic device opened the three security doors that separated the laboratory from the rest of the building. As the doors closed behind them, Lincoln allowed himself a moment to comment.

'There are no Robogs inside this lab,' he said. 'We're safe for the moment.'

The three very quickly made their way to Lincoln's cubicle. There, Boombah lay slumbering in his thick glass cage. Slumbering seemed to be something he was very good at.

'Perhaps we should have discussed this further,' said Simone, looking back towards the security doors nervously. 'Isn't taking property against the law?'

'Bob Santino has no legal claim to Boombah,' said Lincoln. 'Boombah is mine.'

'So why are we taking him at night?'

'Bob Santino may not agree with me.'

'What's a Boombah?' asked Glenn.

Lincoln held up the pink, sleepy cat with something approaching pride in his voice. 'Boombah is my invention. With his genetically modified nose, we'll be able to find the *Dogstar* before . . . anyone else does.'

'How?' asked Simone.

'This is hardly the time to go into details, but to summarize: Boombah can smell dogs from at least five light-years' distance. His presence would be a distinct advantage in our search.'

Boombah miaowed. Simone, who prided herself on her ability to translate, reacted. 'Boombah agrees. But perhaps you should at least tell Mister Santino that you're taking him from the school.'

'Perhaps I should have mentioned this before,' sighed Lincoln. 'Bob Santino doesn't want to rescue the dogs – he wants to destroy them.'

Glenn and Simone stared open-mouthed at Lincoln.

'What?' asked Simone. 'Why?'

'Because they're a threat to his business.'

'You mean . . . he'd kill Hobart, too?' said Simone.

'In a second.'

'But, Linc . . .' stammered Glenn, suddenly feeling very nervous, 'if he's crazy enough to destroy all the dogs, what's he going to do to us if he finds us in here?'

'I could hypothesize,' mused Lincoln, 'but it wouldn't be pretty. Come on.'

At that moment a sound made them freeze. Two sounds, actually – a door opening, and a whiny voice.

' . . . and it's pink. Did I mention that? A mushroomy shade. Well, perhaps mushroom isn't the best description – it's more like the pink you see when the sun sets and . . .'

Dino stopped mid-sentence as the lights came on. There was Lincoln, holding Boombah, with Glenn and Simone standing paralysed beside him.

'Hey!' yelled Santino. 'Put that genetically modified dog-detector down! That's mine!'

'No!' said Lincoln. There was steel in his voice. 'Boombah is legally mine and you can't have him.'

Santino glared at Lincoln, a cold, merciless gleam in his eyes.

'You're a profound disappointment to me, Lincoln.'

'You've had worse,' replied Lincoln, giving Dino a look.

Dino slumped.

Santino's glare intensified. He quickly reached into his pocket and raised something to his lips. An electronic dog whistle! He blew.

At first there was no response. Then the floor started to vibrate. And the walls shook. Suddenly the security doors fell forward and shattered as two Guard-Robogs burst clean through them. Another one burst through the concrete wall to Santino's right. Almost simultaneously, the floor erupted and two more Guard-Robogs burst upwards into the room from the floor below. These Guard-Robogs were the elite unit – shiny black with studded collars. They were large, and deadly.

'Get them!' yelled Santino, and pointed to the Clark children.

Immediately, the children ran in different directions. This wasn't a plan – they simply had no experience working as a team.

The Guard-Robogs leapt after them, drooling synthetic drool and barking synthetic barks. Their jaws were lined with razor-sharp teeth modelled after Great White Sharks. If they caught you, the results were nasty. The kids were fast, but let's face it, they're kids. The Guard-Robogs were state-of-the-art, search-and-destroy automatons.

An hysterical Simone was the first to be trapped. A few cubicles away from Lincoln's, she found herself cornered by a slavering monster. The Guard-Robog stalked closer, sensing its victim was helpless.

Simone screamed.

Luckily for Simone she was in cubicle twenty-four. Her scream made the dog bark-detecting device inside activate. As her scream was around a thousand times louder than the radar gun's tolerance levels (set, incidentally, to detect the bark of a Beagle seven miles away), the feedback was huge. The advancing Guard-Robog vibrated into component parts in seconds.

Santino, meanwhile, was yelling into his wrist-com device, 'Daina! Get up here, now!'

Santino personally took off after Lincoln, his smallish legs pumping with unaccustomed physical exertion.

(Actually, that applied to both chaser and chasee.)

Meanwhile, Glenn was running as fast as he could down a row of cubicles – two Guard-Robogs hot on his heels. These things were tireless, unlike Glenn. His legs were already feeling heavier as the Robogs closed in for the kill. Glenn raced through an area thick with dangling cables from a student's experiment. Busy trying to avoid entanglement in the cables strewn on the floor, Glenn didn't see the thick cable hanging in a loop across his path. As one of the Robogs made a lunge for him, Glenn ran straight into the cable. It looped under his arms. It stretched with his momentum, then picked him up and wrenched him backwards over the Robogs with a bungee-cord action. Glenn was catapulted through the air while the two Robogs slammed into a wall.

Glenn sailed across the laboratory. In desperation, he grabbed at anything to slow his pace. As he passed over cubicle thirty-three, he grasped the dog-detecting X-ray device and held on tight. He was stuck. The cable had him around the shoulders, pulling one way, but his arms held fast. Glenn's hands were sweaty and slippery, and almost immediately his grip began to slide.

'Heeeelllp!' he yelled.

Simone raced past him, pursued by another Guard-Robog. She was hardly in a position to assist. Suddenly, Glenn's hands slipped to the 'on' switch, activating the unperfected X-ray. True to form, the bazooka-like device fired a dog-detecting particle beam at the only dog shape nearby – the Guard-Robog.The particle beam vaporized its target instantly.

Simone looked stunned, but rather than question her good fortune, she took off once more. Rounding the next corner, however, she came face-to-face with Daina!

Daina smiled and cracked her knuckles. One by one.

Meanwhile, Glenn's hands finally slipped and the stretchy cables whipped him away. Once more he sailed helplessly through the air. Passing over cubicle forty-nine, he reached out once more. Sadly, he only managed to grab the cut-out-dog-on-a-stick shape that the student had been using to test his invention with. It didn't help slow Glenn's momentum one little bit.

Glenn shot up into the air, then the cable unwound from around him. For a brief moment, he hung there. Then, as gravity exerted itself, he fell back to the floor. Rather quickly. For a second it looked as if he would land right on top of Daina, but she nimbly stepped aside and reached out instinctively to disarm Glenn in a single fluid move as he fell past her.

Glenn landed with a thud next to Simone. Daina stood there with the dog-cut-out-on-a-stick in her hand.

'Two children versus one ninja-trained bodyguard,' she mused. 'It hardly seems fair.'

She took one step towards them.

Then something lucky happened again.

The newly repaired satellite device in cubicle forty-nine had been activated by the vibration of Glenn hitting the floor. It automatically looked for any dog-like object and pinpointed the dog cut-out shape with its laser. Before Daina could react, the satellite slammed into the cut-out, then her, then the nearby brick wall. When Simone and

Glenn had the courage to look up, all they could see was Daina's legs sticking out of a very large hole in the wall. They also heard a painful moaning sound.

Glenn stood up, smiling at Simone. 'You can thank me later,' he said.

Across the room, Lincoln was running while carrying Boombah. Santino and the largest, meanest-looking Robog were just behind him.

'Grab the kid with the cat. He's the one I want!'

As they raced ahead, Santino suddenly stopped. He quickly raised one hand to bring the Robog to a stop.

Lincoln was standing ahead of him at Dino's cubicle. He was holding Boombah up to something. Boombah's claws were trying to grab it.

'Kindly control your pseudo-animal,' said Lincoln evenly, 'or this painting will be permanently disfigured.'

For the first time, Bob Santino's eyes fell on the portrait of him that Dino had painted. Art critics might say that it was a slightly self-conscious attempt to impart dignity and grandeur to the subject. However, the realization that hit Santino, just as Dino came running up, was that no one had ever painted his portrait before.

'Easy . . . easy . . .' Santino muttered to the Guard-Robogs. Now there were six of them straining to jump on Lincoln. Santino just kept staring at the painting. Lincoln held Boombah towards it once more. Boombah hissed and his claws missed it by centimetres. Maybe Boombah just didn't like figurative work.

'If you increase your proximity, this portrait will resemble confetti,' said Lincoln.

'Did . . . did you paint this, Dino?' asked Santino.

'Yes, Dad. Do you like it?'

Now, Bob Santino is a hard man. Tough, ruthless and mean, too. But the sight of the painting had stirred up feelings in Bob that he couldn't quite explain. For once, he hesitated.

Lincoln saw the moment and pressed his advantage.

'The way I see it, you've got only one choice. Let us leave with *my* property. Now!'

Santino pondered this. He winced as Boombah's claws again swiped the air near his portrait.

'How about I buy the cat off you?' he hissed.

'I'm not open to negotiation. We're going to use Boombah to find the *Dogstar* and save all the dogs. Including our dog Hobart!'

Santino's eyes narrowed. He hated Lincoln even more at that moment.

'Be reasonable, kid. Who needs those mangy mutts? I'm prepared to offer you good money.'

'No way, Santino! Some things are worth more than money!' Lincoln recognized the voice as Simone's. She stepped out of the shadows and joined him.

'You're kidding,' said Santino.

'Especially our dog Hobart!' said Lincoln, putting an end to the matter.

'Nobody says no to Bob Santino!' snarled Santino.

'Get used to it,' was Lincoln's retort.

Santino stood, fuming and indecisive – and getting angrier because he was fuming and indecisive. The Guard-Robogs took a step closer to Lincoln.

'You're not getting away, kid! I want that cat, and as far as I can see, I'm holding all the aces!'

Suddenly, another voice rang out, high above them. It was Glenn.

'That's where you're wrong, big man!'

Glenn was standing on a beam in the roof. He stared down at them and adopted an heroic pose that frankly seemed very unjustified in the current circumstance.

'Yeah?' sneered Santino. 'What are you going to do about it?'

'This!' cried Glenn, and proceeded to tear off his black jumper. Simone immediately put a hand to her forehead.

'Oh no . . .' she muttered.

Underneath, Glenn was wearing his Planet Man top. Even in the artificial light of the lab, its bright red and gold colours shone vividly. The cape fluttered behind him.

Santino simply frowned. Dino, however, looked more impressed.

'Nice top,' he said.

Lincoln was meanwhile adjusting his window-opening device. Unnoticed by the others, the single note it emitted rose higher and higher in pitch until it hit hypersonic and was lost to human auditory senses. No one could hear it, but suddenly the Guard-Robogs started cowering.

'What's wrong with you lot?' yelled Santino. 'Get him!'

But the Guard-Robogs simply whimpered and flattened themselves on the floor.

High above, Glenn smiled triumphantly. 'I knew it!' he cried. 'No one can stand up to a real hero! Let's run!'

Glenn leapt down and Simone and Lincoln joined him.

They ran full tilt towards the shattered doors.

'Stop them! Stop them now!'

But the Robogs didn't move and Daina reappeared holding her aching head. She was limping.

'Get them, Daina! That's what you're paid for!' Santino screamed. Daina, however, simply passed out from the pain of multiple fractures. She fell flat on her face, unconscious. Santino looked up. The Clark kids and Boombah had gone. Santino shook his head. Then he did what generations of dog owners have done when frustrated – he kicked the nearest dog. That being a Guard-Robog with a Dalkinite shell, the pain in Santino's toe was immediate.

Dino decided this was a good time to approach his father with the portrait grasped safely in his hands.

'Luckily that drama ended happily, right, Dad?'

Santino's right eye started twitching.

The back door to the Clark house opened and Simone, Glenn and Lincoln (carrying Boombah) came barrelling in.

'Okay,' said Glenn, 'time to ask Dad.'

The others raced to the *Valiant* while Glenn ran into the workshop where Mark was always tinkering at this time of night.

'Dad, can I borrow the *Valiant*?' he asked.

'Not on your life,' Mark replied, without looking up.

Glenn hesitated, then raced out again.

In the kitchen, he ran straight to Greta.

'Mum, can I borrow the *Valiant* to look for the *Dogstar*?'

Glenn was using the time-honoured technique of hoping that Greta was distracted and using this to his advantage. It turns out she was. She was trying to make banana pudding with Tongan bananas.

'Ask your father,' she replied, absently.

'I did.'

'What did he say?'

'Well, I didn't get the chance to fully explain that I'll be really careful.'

'So, he said no?'

'He didn't say *no*.'

'Well, I know how much Hobart means to you, Glenn . . .'

'Thanks, Mum.'

And Glenn raced out. Again he used the age-old technique of taking any slight parental acknowledgement as a 'yes'.

Greta kept talking, oblivious to the fact that Glenn had left the room.

'. . . and of course he means a lot to me as well. And your father . . . But you've only driven the *Valiant* a handful of times . . . Then there's your homework . . .'

When Glenn reached the Valiant's control room, Simone, Lincoln and Boombah were already waiting.

'Told you. No worries,' said Glenn. 'Let's go!'

As Glenn hit the starter button, the Valiant's aged engines groaned into life. Glenn was strapped into the pilot's seat. Simone was next to him. Lincoln was in the navigator's seat. A sudden movement from behind made them turn.

Gran was strapping herself into a spare seat.

'Gran!' cried Simone. 'What are you doing here?'

'You think I don't miss Hobart, too?' She smiled.

The kids smiled back.

'I've set the navigation coordinates to 2400 by 9, 3, 0, X.2,' said Lincoln. No one had any idea what he meant, but they trusted him.

Glenn instantly hit the launch button.

Mark and Greta came rushing out the front door just as the Valiant's engines gushed white-hot flame. It shot into the air.

'I thought I told that kid!' shouted Mark.

'Mark – you're stifling him,' said Greta.

'Stifling? What about my removals business?'

'They're searching for Hobart. Think of what they'll learn.'

'Greta! I'm worried about their safety!'

'I'm pretty sure your mother's with them.'

'That's what I mean.'

Mark sighed as the *Valiant* passed through the low cover of wispy clouds above the suburb.

At that very moment, Santino's jet-limo came to a sudden halt in the street outside the Clark house.

Hidden gunports slid open, exposing an array of heat-seeking missiles in the side panels. Two missiles suddenly shot up into the air after the *Valiant*.

Lincoln was first to react to the shapes he saw on the screen in front of him.

'Incoming missiles. Initiate evasive manoeuvre!' he yelled.

If there was one thing Glenn was good at, it was evasive manoeuvres. Ever since he'd practised dog-fights with models of Planet Man's flagship versus Karzorkian stealth-fighters when he was young, he'd dreamt of performing them in the Valiant.

In an instant, Glenn jerked back on the controls and threw the ship into a starboard spiral. He simultaneously hit the jet thrusters. If he was expecting the same performance as Planet Man's vessel, he'd be disappointed. The engines backfired and a plasma surge coughed out of them like a burst of super-heated flatulence.

The spiral did, however, cause the two heat-seeking missiles to pass under the ship. As the Valiant sped away, the missiles shot off in separate directions, then turned back to seek more heat. They registered the hottest thing they could find and headed straight towards the dissipating cloud of plasma. They hit each other right in the middle of the cloud.

The resultant explosion rained burning debris down over the suburb below.

Outside the Clark house, Mark and Greta were rendered speechless by what they'd just seen. They turned to the jet-limo just as a rear window was being lowered. Bob Santino waved cheerfully to them from within.

'Sorry,' he called, smiling. 'Hi, folks. Just celebrating the launch with a few fireworks. Hope you don't mind.'

The jet-limo cruised away before Greta or Mark could comment.

The *Valiant* passed out of New Earth's atmosphere quickly.

At his navigation station, Lincoln was looking at a photo. It wasn't the family portrait of all the Clarks with Hobart. This was a smaller shot, just Lincoln cuddling Hobart. In this shot, Gran had managed to capture a rare moment on film. In the photo, Lincoln was smiling.

Lincoln stared at the photo for a few moments before putting it back into his pocket.

In his pilot's seat, Glenn was feeling pretty pleased with himself. 'So much for Bob Santino,' he said. 'Hobart, here we come!'

On the *Dogstar*, Zeke and Alice were walking on D-Deck.

'I think someone will find us soon, Alice,' said Zeke. 'I can feel it in my bones.'

'You mean, in your processing units?'

'No. In my bones.'

'You don't have bones.'

'Yes, I do.'

'No, you don't, Zeke. You're being ridiculous. It's silly for a robot pilot to pretend it's human.'

'I agree with you one hundred per cent, Alice. And there's only one robot pilot on this ship – and that's you. You know something – I feel hungry.'

'You can't feel hungry.'

'I feel like food, Alice. How terribly human of me. I'm going to program the food synthesizer to whip me up . . . some fruit!'

Zeke turned round and headed for the lift that led to the bridge. Alice followed.

It was ironic, really. They turned just before reaching Hobart's quarters. If they had taken just a couple more steps, they would have noticed that the laser bars to his kennel were turned off and that it was vacant.

'This is going to be interesting,' said Alice drily as they headed back to the lift.

'I agree, Alice. You're very perceptive for a robot.'

Alice shook her head. Both of them stepped inside.

As the *Valiant* soared through space, Boombah looked out from the very front of the ship. Right at the pointy end. The frontal nose-cone had now been modified by Lincoln. What was previously a forward observation area, suitable for one person, had now been provided with a large pillow for Boombah to recline on. (Reclining was another thing Boombah seemed to do very easily.)

Boombah blinked lazily as he looked out at the inky blackness ahead of them. If he was interested, it didn't show. If he was aware of his importance to the success of their mission, it wasn't apparent.

As he clawed his pillow to make it more comfortable, his actions were being watched by the Clark kids and Gran on the video monitor on the bridge.

'Boombah's position will allow him maximum exposure to any faint traces of odours out there,' announced Lincoln to the others. 'If a dog comes within five light-years, Boombah will detect it.'

'How will we know that?' asked Gran.

'Boombah will behave like any normal cat. He'll become agitated and act defensively. And this B-Cam will immediately inform us of any change in behaviour.'

The kids looked at the screen. Boombah was now lying down, virtually asleep.

'He doesn't look as if he's searching for anything,' noted Simone.

'He doesn't have to search. He just has to sit there. His instincts will do the work. Even if he's asleep, he'll react.'

On the audio link to B-Cam, Boombah let out a small miaow before starting to snore.

'He says he likes it here,' observed Simone.

Next to Simone, Glenn smiled. He was feeling confident now. Out here, in space, piloting the *Valiant*, he had a feeling that destiny was calling.

'This is great,' he said. 'We're on a mission – just like Planet Man.' Simone shook her head but Glenn continued. 'With Lincoln's brain, and my heroic instincts, we can't fail, right, Planet Man?'

On the dashboard next to his controls, Glenn had placed his Planet Man doll. Its eyes lit up as a pre-recorded answer emerged.

'Heroes aren't born – *Glenn* – they're made. They're made by deeds. Although sometimes they're born.'

'That's so true,' said Glenn.

'I'm beginning to wonder if I should ever have bought you your first Planet Man comic,' mused Gran fatalistically.

What was that noise? It woke me up. Maybe it was one of the machine-things down here. It feels like I'm a long way down inside the kennel. There aren't any dogs here. Maybe I shouldn't have climbed out of the small corridor. I don't like it here. I think I'll just grab my toy and . . . Oh, no! It's gone!

That's not possible! It was here when I fell asleep. I put it right here.

Something snuck up and took it! But how? My ears are really good. My nose is really sharp. Nothing could just sneak up on me and steal my favourite toy!

I thought I'd have it forever. Then again, I always thought I'd have my pack forever too. Mark, Greta, Gran, Simone, Glenn and Lincoln . . . Mark, Greta, Gran, Simone, Glenn and Lincoln.

Here's a moving-room – like the one back home. There's an arrow going up and down. I know this! You hop into the room and you go up. Let's see where it goes.

On the bridge of the *Dogstar*, Zeke and Alice stood in front of the food synthesizer. Zeke dexterously pressed some symbols on the touch-screen display.

'You're going to regret this, Zeke,' said Alice.

'I doubt that very much. I've asked the synthesizer for a light, refreshing snack.'

In two seconds, a banana slid out of a slot. Zeke picked it up and looked at it suspiciously.

'What is it?' asked Alice.

'The synthesizer says it's a banana from Tongatapu – well, obviously not a real one – a synthetic copy. But so close you can't tell the difference. Ahhh, yes. I'm going to enjoy this.'

Zeke started to slide the banana (unpeeled) into his mouth opening; an opening designed exclusively to project his voice. Alice just shook her head.

The moving-room has taken me . . . where? I don't think I've been up into this part of the big kennel. It's different up here. There are no dogs here either. There're just lots more strange machines making funny noises.

I think I'd better go back to the little corridor. It's safer in there with the wires and pipes.

There's a grille – right – in I go.

I can't see my toy anywhere. And that's sad.

Once I lost it, and Greta found it and gave it back to me. But that time it smelt really bad when I got it back. It smelt like Glenn and Simone and Lincoln's clothes after Greta washes them. All the good grotty smells were gone.

So I rolled it in dirt and mud until it smelt good again.

But, now – no smell – and no toy. I wish Glenn or Simone or Lincoln were here to find it for me. They'd know where to look.

Mark, Greta, Gran, Simone, Glenn and Lincoln. Mark, Greta, Gran, Simone, Glenn and Lincoln.

What's that?

There're the two big-dolls. Thank goodness I'm behind this grille where they can't see me. Clever Hobart. Good Hobart.

What's the loud big-doll doing? It's stuffing manch into its mouth, but it's going everywhere.

It's spilling it on the floor. It can't even get all the manch into its mouth. Why doesn't it chew? Bad big-doll! Glenn always gets in trouble if he spills his manch. Is big-doll like Glenn? No. I don't think so. It doesn't have a nice smell.

Now it's got manch smeared all over its face and all over the floor. What a waste.

Wait – here they come!

The little cleaner-toys. Hundreds of them. Gee, they're quick. They really don't like a mess. They're picking up all the bits of manch on the floor and taking it away.

Now they're running up the big-doll's legs to its face and picking bits of manch off. That's horrible.

I'm going. I don't like the big-dolls and I don't like those cleaner-things. I'm staying away from them.

I'll squeeze through here . . .

As Hobart squeezed past a relay console in the duct, he had to push really hard. It was a small space to get through, but he made it and continued his journey.

What he didn't notice was that a few hairs were shed during this manoeuvre. They floated through the air, and a couple of them wafted through the grille below the relay.

They then entered the corridor where Alice was watching the cleaner-bots remove the mess Zeke had made.

'Very tasty,' Zeke was insisting. 'And so filling.'

'You're a very stupid robot,' said Alice, unimpressed.

At that moment, three of Hobart's hairs hit the floor of the corridor. Immediately, twenty of the cleaner-bots converged on them. In a jumble of electronic squeaks and squawks, they discussed the significance of those hairs among themselves. They were very concerned. These things weren't meant to be here.

Zeke was pretending not to understand the cleaner-bot discussion. But all robots are programmed with connectivity devices. Alice understood their concerns immediately.

They finished debating the significance of the hairs. They had concluded that their presence indicated a pest infestation aboard the ship. The collective pseudo-consciousness that linked all the millions of cleaner-bots on the *Dogstar* agreed. They immediately informed the pilots via wireless-com-protocol.

Alice reacted as she received the message.

'Did you hear that, Zeke?'

'Hear what, Alice?'

'Don't be silly, Zeke.'

'Oh – I see what's happening. You can hear the cleaner-bots because you're a robot. I'm a human. Of course I can't hear them. Funny, isn't it?'

A fuming Alice stormed off to the central security

controls. She immediately pushed a large, red button.

One hundred and three levels below, in a dark room, a red light turned to green. Below this light, a hatch door suddenly slid open with a hiss.

The room behind it was small, but occupied. A dark shape stirred. Two eyes glowed in the darkness.

The shape stepped out of the room into the light of the corridor on six mechanical legs. It was another robot – but a dangerous-looking one. It stood about half as tall again as Hobart and its sleek lines reeked of ruthless menace. It was a 'Pest-Exterminator Mark IX'.

It paused for a moment, taking in different readings from the air around it. Gathering data. A small tube immediately extended from its face and seemed to sniff the floor nearby.

It froze as it detected a scent.

Then slowly, calmly, the Pest-Exterminator Mark IX moved off down the corridor, following the scent. It was on the trail of the pest that had infiltrated the *Dogstar*. Its job was simple. Kill.

On the *Valiant*, Glenn's initial rush of 'take-off adrenaline' was fading. The reality that this search might not yield instant results was just starting to filter into his consciousness. He was beginning to realize that it's hard to be dramatic when you're doing a routine, sector-by-sector search of the entire universe. Looking at instruments and checking the B-Cam monitor just don't lend themselves to heroic actions.

Alone on the bridge and feeling bored, Glenn was surprised when an old memory surfaced. One day, long ago, Glenn had become extremely distraught when he couldn't find his Planet Man figurine anywhere. He'd looked high and low, but it had simply vanished. What he didn't know was that Greta had accidentally thrown it out in the rubbish. What he also didn't know was that Hobart made a habit of picking through the rubbish before it was collected. Hobart came across Glenn's doll and, recognizing it, brought it straight back to him.

Glenn was overjoyed at being reunited with his toy, but also severely embarrassed by how much he had wept uncontrollably earlier in the day. He resolved never to cry in front of his parents again.

Glenn sighed as he looked at the same Planet Man figurine standing on his console.

'So, Planet Man, do you think we'll ever see Hobart again?'

The doll's eyes lit up.

'A true hero – *Glenn* – never gives . . .'

The voice died. The batteries perhaps?

'What's that, Planet Man? A true hero never gives what? Money?'

The doll tried again. 'A true hero never gives . . .'

But again the voice died.

'Flowers?'

'A true hero never gives up, idiot!' snarled Simone from the door of his cabin.

'Oh . . . Simone,' said Glenn as he hid the doll behind his back. 'I was just . . . singing.'

'You were talking to your doll.'

'Action figurine, Simone!'

'I don't want to argue,' she sighed. 'Lincoln wants us to see something – on the bridge.'

Moments later, Glenn and Simone found themselves watching Hank Henry interviewing Bob Santino on a USI transmission. Lincoln was replaying an item he'd just watched.

'I'm here with Bob Santino. Are you sure I can't call you Bob?'

'Quite sure, Hank,' said Santino.

'Very well. I believe you have another fascinating announcement for us, Mister Santino.'

'Yes, I do, Hank – Dino, if you please?'

Santino and Hank stood staring at Dino (dressed very smartly in maroon velour) who stood off to one side. Dino was still frozen, however, staring at the camera with his fixed smile, seemingly mesmerized.

'Dino . . . ?'

No response.

'Dino!' Santino yelled.

Both Dino and Hank jumped. Dino quickly rushed to a long cord hanging nearby. He pulled on it.

Behind Hank and Santino, curtains parted. It now became clear that the broadcast was coming direct from Santino's corporate headquarters – in Santino's office.

Behind them was a window looking out into a large hangar – a construction area. But it was what was in the construction area that caught everyone's attention – a huge, sleek-looking spaceship – twenty, perhaps thirty times bigger than the *Valiant*.

On the *Valiant*, the Clark kids reacted as the camera tracked over the surface of the ship. It was extremely fast. You could tell that much just by looking at it. Buzzing around it were workers – some with jet-packs, some on floating platforms. They were putting the finishing touches to the craft.

Glenn, Simone and Lincoln looked even more worried as they watched the broadcast.

'Wow. Not even Planet Man has a ship like that,' mused Glenn.

'Planet Man isn't real,' said Simone.

'Is so!'

'Quiet!' said Lincoln. His face looked serious. (Then again, his face always looked serious.) 'With that new ship, Santino has become an even more formidable adversary.'

'What does that mean?' Glenn whispered to Simone. She ignored him.

'I call her the BobCat – not bad, eh?' preened Santino.

'It's very impressive, Mister Santino,' replied Hank.

'It's more than that, Hank. It's the fastest ship in the Galaxy. It's well known that Bob Santino spares no expense for excellence and this is no exception. I've hired the best designers and the best builders and paid them top dollar – top dollar, Hank – to build me the most advanced ship of its kind. There's not a ship in the known universe that can hold a candle to this baby.'

'It looks tremendous. Um . . . why did you build it, Mister Santino?'

'With this masterpiece, I intend to find the missing *Dogstar* and return it to New Earth.'

'But Mister Santino – once people get their dogs back, surely there won't be any demand for your Robogs?'

Very consciously, Santino stood patting the Robog at his feet. He turned it to a slightly more flattering angle.

'You mean the superb robotic dog, manufactured by my company SRC, and the source of my immense wealth?'

'That's the one.'

Santino took a deep breath. He placed his hand over his heart as the camera moved in for a close-up.

'There comes a time, Hank,' said Santino, very gravely, 'when we must put the concerns of humanity before finance. As with my School for the Gifted, I'm deeply committed to finding those poor, lost doggies. It's simply my way of "giving back", Hank.'

'So why the guns?'

Santino hesitated. Close-ups of the ship clearly showed gunports bristling with a variety of highly sophisticated weaponry.

'They're not guns,' smiled Santino.

'What are they?'

'Ahhh . . . navigational aids.'

Suddenly, one of the guns fired. A burst of explosive energy hit a floating construction platform with many welders working on it. The platform exploded and the workers fell several storeys to the floor of the hangar.

Dino's head popped out of the cockpit.

'Sorry, Father . . .' he stammered, as he saw the workers on the floor below twitching and moaning.

'Dino! How many times have I told you? Don't fire the navigational aids unless I say so.'

Santino turned back and smiled winningly at Hank. Hank tried to maintain his own unflappable grin. There was a worried look in his eyes, however.

Lincoln looked grave. 'We're no match for that ship. It's faster, more manoeuvrable and it has weapons. We have none. If Santino were to find us before we find the *Dogstar*, I calculate our chances of surviving the encounter at under three per cent.'

'Still,' said Simone, 'it looks like it's not quite finished. We've still got time before he launches it.'

'He launched it ten minutes ago,' announced Lincoln.

'So what will happen if Santino finds us before he finds the *Dogstar*?' asked Glenn.

'If I were him, firstly I'd disable us, then I'd take Boombah, then I'd destroy us.'

Glenn and Simone looked miserable.

'Don't worry,' said Lincoln. 'The chances of him finding us are probably twenty million to one. Provided we don't give off any signals that he can trace.'

'What sort of signals?'

'Oh, say, microwaves for example.'

It's not the first time we've talked about ironic utterances seemingly foreshadowing coincidental actions. Another one of these was about to happen. A brief second after Lincoln uttered the word 'microwaves', the kids heard the unmistakable 'ding' of a microwave oven finishing a cooking cycle. Then Gran entered carrying a bowl of steaming hot popcorn.

'You're never too old for popcorn,' she laughed. 'Anybody want some?'

She couldn't understand why they had turned white.

As fate would have it, the *BobCat*, with Daina at the controls, was now cruising a mere two light-years' distance from the *Valiant*. Daina instantly reacted to an energy spike signal on one of her many sophisticated-because-they're-expensive instruments.

'A microwave signal has been detected from a small removals craft in the Magpie Cluster. Five life-forms aboard. Four human. One mutant feline.'

'It must be the *Valiant*!' cried Santino, rubbing his hands together in the customary 'evil adversary' style. He was taking to the part like a natural.

'Yay!' said Dino.

'Dino, don't be immature,' snarled Santino.

'The *Valiant* will be in firing range in five universal minutes,' said Daina.

'Yay!' shouted Santino.

And the *BobCat* leapt into hyperspace.

Four universal minutes and fifty universal seconds later, a warning alarm sounded on Lincoln's console.

'The scanner indicates a large, fast vessel matching the

BobCat's architecture emerging from hyperspace on an intercept course. This could get ugly,' said Lincoln.

The ship shuddered suddenly as a photon bolt just missed it and exploded ahead of them.

'Battle Stations!' yelled Glenn.

'This is a removals ship!' shouted Simone. 'We don't have Battle Stations!'

'Or weapons,' sighed Gran. 'Unless you count bubble wrap.'

The *Valiant* shuddered, rocked by a second explosion nearby. Paint blistered on its aged hull from the white-hot heat.

On the *BobCat,* Santino chortled gleefully.

'Don't destroy the *Valiant,* Daina. Just immobilize it. I must get my hands on that mutant cat!'

The crew of the Valiant were holding on to anything they could grab as explosions rocked their ship. Simone pushed a button and Boombah was sucked from the nose-cone on to the bridge via a vacuum tube. Simone clutched him as he emerged. He miaowed fretfully.

'Boombah's saying he's scared.'

'Thanks, Simone,' shouted Glenn, fighting the ship's controls. 'That's really helpful.'

'Boombah also says that you're a baby who takes advice from a doll!'

Glenn didn't have time to respond. He put the *Valiant* into a series of rolls and dives, trying to keep away from Daina's weapons. But the *BobCat* was right on their tail.

Daina was good. But then again, Santino always did buy the best.

'I just thought of a great plan all by myself,' yelled Glenn, suddenly. 'We can ram the *BobCat*!'

'What with?'

'The *Valiant*, of course!' yelled Glenn, as a burst of laser-cannon singed the port-side window.

Simone was incredulous. 'Ram this old tub into a brand-new battle cruiser that's thirty times bigger than us?'

'It has the element of surprise.'

'With the added bonus of stupidity.'

As Glenn kept swerving the ship from side to side, desperately trying to stay out of the *BobCat*'s firing line, Lincoln's eyes never left the scanner in front of him.

'Fire now! Fire now!' cried Santino, who was on his feet and standing directly behind Daina's pilot seat, prodding her.

'Yes, sir.'

'Faster, Daina! Use the thermo-torpedoes!'

'Yes, sir.'

'I have an idea,' said Lincoln over the commotion aboard the Valiant. 'I suggest we fly into that asteroid field.'

Lincoln pointed to the starboard quarter. In the near distance was a large asteroid field. There were millions of them – a chaotic cloud, thick with irregular-shaped rocks. There looked to be no easy path through.

'Are you crazy?' yelled Glenn. 'We'll be smashed to bits!'

'That is a statistical possibility. However, the probability of the *BobCat* suffering worse damage is proportional to its increased size. Also, we have one thing on this ship that can minimize the risk of damage to ourselves.'

'Planet Man?' asked Glenn.

'No. Bubble wrap! Head for the asteroids!'

Glenn threw the craft into a tight turn.

'What are they doing?' screamed Santino as Daina kept pace with the *Valiant*'s course.

'I'm not sure, sir,' replied Daina.

As the *Valiant* surged towards the asteroids, large, mechanical arms emerged from ports in the hull. Enormous rolls of bubble wrap were attached to them. These wrapping arms, last used by Mark to wrap up a Tongatapuan temple, started swirling the bubble wrap round the hull of the *Valiant*. As aged as this technology was, the task was completed just as the ship entered the cloud of rocks.

'They're entering the asteroid field, Daina!' yelled Santino. 'We can't follow them there!'

'I'll disable their engines first!' cried Daina as she fired off a barrage of photon bolts at the fleeing vessel. The shots missed, rebounding off smaller asteroids and smashing them to pieces.

The *Valiant* crew were buffeted by vibrations as shattered asteroid chunks bounced off the bubble-wrapped hull. Glenn kept his eyes on the path ahead, swerving dexterously around chunks of rock as they appeared in front of him.

A few thermo-torpedoes blew more asteroids to bits in spectacular pyrotechnics, but the bubble wrap stood firm. The *Valiant* was dented, but no hull breaches were registering on Lincoln's instruments.

Santino was fuming. Daina threw up her hands as the Valiant was lost from sight in the asteroid field.

'It's no good, Mister Santino. I can't get a clear shot.'

'Never mind, Daina. They obviously think they can survive an asteroid field – I'm betting they can't. Stop all engines.'

Glenn was still forging ahead at a steady pace. Now and again, smaller asteroids bounced off the protected hull, but Glenn managed to stay clear of the large ones.

On the bridge, Gran picked herself up off the floor. She looked aghast as she saw one of her legs lying a few feet away.

'My leg! It's come off.'

'Gran, that's the spare one I made for you last week,' said Lincoln, picking it up and taking it to a storage compartment.

'Oh yes, silly me,' said Gran. She looked down. Both of her legs were intact and attached.

'Did you see that?' crowed Glenn. 'Did you see the way I outclassed the fastest ship in the Galaxy? Did you see the skill? The nerve? Planet Man would have been proud of me.'

'If he was real. Which he isn't,' muttered Simone.

'You've been a very good boy, Glenny,' said Gran, ruffling his hair. 'I always said you took after your grandfather.'

'Thanks, Gran.'

'Mind you, he couldn't fly a kite,' she said. 'And he was so short-sighted, *he* couldn't see an oncoming disaster, either.'

'What do you mean?' said Glenn, just as he turned back to find out why the light coming through the windows had gone dark.

Looming ahead of them was the largest, lumpiest asteroid in the universe. It had been detected seconds earlier by Lincoln's instruments, but because Lincoln was still putting Gran's spare leg away in a locker, he hadn't spotted it on his screen. Perhaps he foolishly assumed that Glenn would still be looking straight ahead, rather than bragging about his own brilliance.

Whatever the contributing factors, the inescapable fact was that a huge asteroid was now too close for Glenn to possibly avoid. Already it blotted out the entire windscreen's view.

'Brace for impact!' screamed Simone.

Mercifully, Glenn fainted moments before the *Valiant* crashed.

Glenn was the last to wake up. As he looked around, his head stopped spinning and he heard groans coming from the others. Simone was rubbing her neck. Lincoln was pulling himself to his feet. Gran was reattaching a cybernetic hand to her left arm.

'What happened?' Glenn asked.

The *Valiant* had crashed headlong into the large asteroid without slowing down. It hit the asteroid at a twenty-two-degree angle to its surface. The bubble-wrap, however, caused the ship to bounce, and bounce, and bounce, end over end. It skidded a quarter of the way round the asteroid's circumference before coming to a halt. This would all show up much later on Lincoln's analysis of the data from the flight recorder, but for now, Lincoln's reply was brief.

'We crashed,' he said simply.

Simone gently retrieved Boombah from where he had landed. He looked dazed, but all right. His thick, pink fur and rotund shape were his own equivalent of bubble wrap.

'Boombah's all right. No thanks to you, Glenn.'

'It's not my fault.'

'You were the pilot! Whose fault is it supposed to be?'

'You're always blaming me!'

'Because you're always doing something stupid!'

'Stop her, Gran!'

'Don't shout at your brother, Simone,' said Gran. 'He never listens anyway.'

Lincoln was studying his instruments too intently to get involved with a trivial sibling dispute.

'According to these readings,' he said, 'we're still in the middle of the asteroid field. I believe we've crash-landed on a large asteroid in the very centre of the field. The asteroid has enough gravity to sustain a weak atmosphere.'

'It looks ugly,' said Glenn.

'So do you,' sniped Simone.

Lincoln refused to be drawn into this pettiness. He continued: 'Much of the bubble wrap has come undone and the automatic dispenser is wrecked. Someone will have to go outside and replace the bubble wrap by hand.'

'I'll do it,' said Glenn immediately.

'Let me check the oxygen level first.'

'No time for that! As Planet Man says – adventure waits for no one.'

He emerged from the Valiant moments later, a cumbersome figure, totally sealed in a bulky Vacuum Suit. He looked around with a very heroic expression on his face.

'That's one small step for man, one giant leap for . . .'

' . . . a baby who talks to dolls!' said Simone, stepping out from the doorway behind him. Lincoln and Gran appeared.

They were all stepping out on to the surface wearing nothing but their normal clothes. Glenn looked puzzled.

'The oxygen level is suitable for humans,' said Lincoln, coolly.

Glenn immediately raised the visor on his helmet.

'I was about to say that,' he muttered.

Gran looked around at the inhospitable horizon. The asteroid was rather bleak – just rocky outcrops and dusty plains. It didn't have a lot going for it.

'What a dump,' said Gran. 'I've seen more interesting dirt in Hobart's litter box.'

At the mention of Hobart's name, everyone took a moment. There was a beat of silence before Simone said what they were all thinking.

'I wonder how he is?'

It looks safe to come out, now. There's no one around.

Aghhh . . . it's a tight fit getting through this grille, but there . . . I'm back in the big hallway. Now there's room to move. I can stretch. Ahhh.

Which way? Everything is the same wherever I go. Millions of dogs in kennels. All looking sad, like me. And none of them can tell me where I am.

I'm not going near the big-dolls again. I don't trust them. They're not like my pack.

My pack.

Something tells me they're not here in this big kennel. I hope someone's doing my jobs or they'll be in trouble. I hope . . .

What was that?

The Pest-Exterminator Mark IX had been busy. With cold precision it had unerringly tracked the scent it was following up fourteen decks and through one hundred and twenty-two separate holds. It never deviated for a moment from relentless-pursuit mode. Thermal imaging and bio-aura sensors warned that its prey was close at hand. All available weapons suddenly switched to the highest state of readiness.

There it is again.

Where's the sound coming from? I can't see anything.

Aghhh! Something's grabbed me!

It's got me round the gumble. Fang into it! Oww! It's hard! It's grabbed my foot, too! I'll roll. And again! No. It's still got me. Owww!

Fang into this cable – it's softer. It breaks. There! Take that!

It's too fast! It's slamming me into the wall! It's coming for me again. But I can grab it, too! There! One of its legs is in my mouth. It can hit me as much as it likes, but I'm not letting go!!

What's that smell? Gas? It smells like someone spraying flea spray in a room. Is it spraying gas at me? But I can hold my breath. I can shake this thing!

There! Its leg has come off! I've gotta run. Maybe it's not as fast without a leg. Aghhh!

It caught me again! It's still got five other legs. Incredible! What's that? A needle? Where did that come from? It's coming from inside its body – coming at me! Just like the vet! No way am I letting that happen again!

Fang it! Fang it again! And again! There, it's loosened its grip. Now push! There – it's gone over that railing. Run! Run! Run!

Where was that grille? Up here somewhere. There!

Quick! Inside. Hide. Wuzza!! It can't follow me here! It's too big!

Calm down. Don't breathe too loud. Keep quiet. Good dog. Good dog.

I can't hear it. I've lost it.

Safe for now . . .

What was that thing?

On the asteroid, Lincoln was examining the bubble wrap round the *Valiant*. In places it had come away completely and was trailing out behind the ship in the dirt. However, quite a lot was intact, a significant tribute to its durability.

'This will take some time to repair,' noted Lincoln.

'Do you think anyone's ever been here before?' asked Simone, looking around at the desolate rock.

'That's unlikely,' replied Lincoln. 'Passage through the asteroid field is highly perilous. No ships would attempt it unless they were in dire straits. Like us. I think it's safe to say we're the first visitors to this area.'

'Do you think it's inhabited?' asked Simone.

'It's an asteroid!' smirked Glenn. 'Of course it's not inhabited.'

'Then who are they?' asked Gran, pointing to several figures in the distance.

First contact between alien races is always a tricky thing. Both sides tend to stand off, waiting for the other to make a move. There's always a doubt; a tiny worry in the back of your mind that they might not like you. That maybe your clothes look funny to them. That maybe you've inadvertently insulted them with some innocent gesture already. First meetings tend to be slow affairs – each side feeling each other out gently.

Glenn Clark, however, had no subtlety about him at all.

As soon as he saw the primitive-looking, green, scaly-skinned humanoids with tails, he waved and called out.

'Hi there! How's it going? Oh, yeah – we come in peace and all that stuff.'

He was immediately struck by a rock thrown by one of the aliens. It hit him square on the helmet of his Vacuum Suit.

'Ow!' said Glenn, and fell flat on his back.

'That was a good shot,' mused Gran in admiration.

'We should be careful here,' whispered Lincoln. 'Try not to do anything to offend them.'

Simone smiled. For some reason, she was feeling confident as well. 'I'll try using Ultraspeak. It is a universal language, after all.' She called out. 'Klaatu blong tutu blong sahu.'

The reaction was instantaneous. Immediately, every member of the small group of aliens started picking up rocks and throwing them as hard as they could at the visitors. Gran was right. They were very good shots. Each hit was bang-on something important: a nerve, a joint, a major muscle. As the Clarks' bodies went numb, it was obvious they were helpless against this primitive fire-power.

Once more, everything went black.

Bob Santino was pacing backwards and forwards on the bridge of the *BobCat*. Patience had never been one of Bob's strong points, and now it was being sorely tested.

'We could play charades,' suggested Dino.

'No, Dino.'

'We could play "I Spy".'

'No, Dino.'

'We could try counting the stars and . . .'

'Don't talk while Daddy's thinking, Dino. There's a good boy.'

Santino returned to pacing and looking out the window at the millions of asteroids stretching as far as the eye could see ahead of the stationary *BobCat*.

'But how do I know when you're thinking, Father?'

'If I'm breathing, I'm thinking, Dino. Count on it.'

Dino thought about this carefully as he watched his father pacing. Something about this statement bothered him. He took a few moments to realize what it was.

'But that would mean I can't *ever* talk to you.'

'Funny thing, that,' muttered Santino.

Daina took the opportunity to break the monotony.

'Sir, I think there's a good chance the *Valiant* has been destroyed in the asteroid field. My instruments aren't detecting any movement in there.'

'If I relied on instruments, Daina,' said Santino, 'where do you think I'd be now? I'd be nowhere. The only things I rely on are my instincts. And those instincts are telling me to wait.'

Daina didn't argue. She settled in for the long haul. Unaccustomed to reading to while away the hours, or even, say, doing a crossword, Daina settled for cracking her knuckles.

One by one.

Slowly.

Dino winced with every crack.

As feeling returned to the Clark kids' limbs, they found themselves in a rather shabby prison cell. When the aliens had stopped throwing rocks, the kids and Gran found they were numb all over. They couldn't move. Such was the accuracy of the aliens' throws, however, that their bodies were not bruised. As the numbness affecting their arms and legs wore off, they found themselves able to move freely inside the cell with no ill effects from their pelting.

'Simone?' asked Gran, delicately. 'Exactly what did you say to those aliens?'

'Klaatu blong tutu blong sahu.'

'What does it mean?'

'We are your friends.'

'It doesn't mean "please throw rocks at us and put us in jail"?'

'No.'

'I wonder why they did it then.'

The Clarks were suddenly silent as a door opened nearby. A small group of aliens entered and stared at their captives. The aliens were short, about as tall as Glenn. They wore simple, somewhat shabby clothes and had green scaly skin, sharp teeth and a prominent tail. After their last experience, each of the Clarks made a silent choice not to say anything unless they were spoken to.

The four aliens held a muted discussion among themselves, then left one of their number alone with the prisoners.

As soon as the others left, the alien walked to the bars of the cell and stared in at the strangers. It was hard to tell what it was thinking. It was an alien after all.

For a while, no one spoke. Then Simone summoned up all her courage. She made another attempt at Ultraspeak.

'Klaatu blong tutu bing alta vista blog google yahoo.'

The alien stared at her for a long moment.

'If you must know, we lift our tails out of the way,' the alien replied.

'You speak English?' cried Simone.

Funny, isn't it, how so many alien races separated by vast distances across space seem to speak English. This quirk of fate seems unlikely on the surface, but many science-fiction writers have described this quite accurately. Critics may well be sceptical, but the truth is, the Universe does have a habit of helping out.

'What's your name?' Simone asked.

'Gemma,' said the alien.

'A girl! That's a pretty name,' said Gran.

'It means "one who eats eyeballs".'

'Nice,' said Glenn.

'You,' said Gemma to Glenn.

'Me?'

'Yes, you are clearly the leader.'

Glenn smiled. This was good. A smart alien.

'I see you recognize natural leadership qualities,' he said.

'No, you're the biggest,' Gemma observed.

Actually, this was a mistake. Because Glenn was still wearing his Vacuum Suit, he looked much bigger and bulkier than the others. Gemma wasn't to know he was shorter than Gran and Simone.

'You have the most meat on you,' the alien continued. 'You clearly dominate your tribe and get the largest portions of food.'

'Well, she got that right,' muttered Simone.

'You will tell your tribe that resistance is useless,' Gemma continued. 'You will remain here until you have served the sentence for your crime.'

'What crime?' cried Simone. 'All I did was say "Klaatu blong tutu blong sahu". I was being friendly.'

'Since when is it friendly to tell someone to sit on a cactus?'

'Nice going, Simone,' said Glenn. He turned back to Gemma. 'You can't keep us here. We demand a fair trial.'

'There are no trials here. Only punishment.'

'Who says so?' cried Glenn.

'It's the law of Gavin,' said the alien.

'I'm not scared of someone named Gavin. Bring him out! Let me talk to him.'

'You want to talk to Gavin?'

'Yes.'

'Gavin is the name of our planet, you moron.'

Glenn thought about this for a moment. Had he been insulted? Probably. This little alien was asking for it.

'Think you're smart, do you?' he said.

'Smarter than you,' she replied.

'Glenn – please be quiet and don't aggravate the situation.'

Lincoln had stepped forward. He had been conspicuously silent so far, but now, after carefully observing the alien, he had decided he might have a better chance of sensible dialogue with her.

'There's been a mistake,' said Lincoln calmly through the bars to Gemma. 'My sister made a rudimentary error in translation. That is hardly the basis of a serious crime. Reason and common sense dictate that both our peoples would benefit more from communication than conflict. Release us and we can show you many things that will help your society.'

This all sounded very sensible, but at that moment Lincoln was standing very close to the bars of the cell. He wasn't expecting Gemma to grab him by the nose, which is exactly what she did. She gave it a painful tweak.

'Ahhh ahhhh,' yelled Lincoln before the alien finally released it.

'Hah!' said Gemma. 'First lesson – don't get too close to me! That was fun!'

Lincoln backed off, rubbing his nose.

Gemma did a little celebratory dance and picked up a rock from the floor. She casually threw it at an insect buzzing down the hallway. The rock hit the insect, squashing it against the wall.

'Great shot,' said Gran, admiringly.

'Throwing rocks is our national sport,' said Gemma. 'Also our national dance.'

'Do you practise a lot?'

'Oh yes. Every day. The tribe will all be practising together later this afternoon.'

'That's a lovely idea,' smiled Gran.

'Yes. We need to be good. Because tomorrow you will be pelted with rocks until you beg for mercy.'

The Clarks frowned as they heard this news.

'If we begged for mercy now,' asked Glenn, 'could we skip the rock pelting altogether?'

'Sorry. No.'

'But you don't understand,' said Lincoln, making sure he was well back from the bars this time. 'We are on a vitally important mission to find the missing *Dogstar*.'

'What's that?'

'It's a huge Space Ark full of dogs.'

'Dogs? What are dogs?'

'Canines. Quadrupeds. Four-legged animals.'

'Ah, I understand,' said Gemma. 'Food.'

Gran stepped forward. 'No, not food. They're pets.'

'Pets? We don't have that word on Gavin.'

'See?' said Gran, taking a photo from her pocket. It was the last family photo with Hobart. She looked at it fondly.

'This is Hobart – our pet. He's aboard the *Dogstar*, lost in space somewhere, and we want him back.'

'And that's why we can't hang around for you to throw rocks at us,' said Glenn. 'Not that we're not flattered.'

Suddenly, Gemma grabbed the photo. Gran was aghast.

'You can't have that!'

'Yes, I can.'

'No, you can't!' said Lincoln. He was standing near the bars now, and as Gemma turned, he grabbed the photo back off her. Gemma was surprised – and somehow delighted. Her eyes narrowed.

'Give me that!' she snarled.

'No way!' said Lincoln, stepping backwards to the centre of the cell and out of her reach.

'But I want it!'

Glenn immediately grabbed the photo from Lincoln and stood up to his full height in the Vacuum Suit.

'Over my dead body,' he announced.

He wasn't prepared for what happened next. Gemma suddenly opened the door of the cell with a key, and stepped inside. She was smiling a slightly disconcerting smile.

'You want to fight to the death for the object?' she asked.

'Ahhh . . . that isn't quite what I meant,' said Glenn.

'Are you scared to fight me, enormous one?'

'I'm not scared of anything!'

Perhaps emboldened by his protective Vacuum Suit, Glenn adopted a martial-arts pose he'd learned from the Planet Man TV series. He felt cool, almost confident.

In two seconds that didn't matter, however, as Gemma

used her tail like a lasso, whipped it round Glenn's legs and threw him to the ground. He hit hard, and the photo flew out of his hands.

When the dust had cleared, Glenn was horizontal and unconscious and Gemma had the Clark family's favourite photo in her green, scaly hands.

The conscious Clarks were horrified.

That metal-monster was fast. But I hurt it more than it hurt me. It won't get me again.

Where's a door in this place? Or a window? There – up ahead – another grille. I'll be able to see out into the big hall.

I can see up and down the corridor outside. But there's nothing. Wait . . . What's that smell? It couldn't be . . .? Could it? My toy! If that's my toy, I'll be a good dog for-ever! Promise!

If I open this grille – a little push – there. Now, careful. Not too fast. I really hope it's my toy. I think I can smell it just round the corner.

Follow your nose. Follow your nose. Nearly there . . .

I see it! There it is, just at the end of the hall. It's just sitting there. It looks the same. Is it safe? I think so. I'll take it back into the small corridor. We'll both be safe there.

Now I've got it in my mouth. It's just the right taste.

But how did it . . . ?

Aghhh! The monster! It was waiting for me! It put my toy here to trap me! And I've fallen into the trap! Aghhh! It hurts! Let go of me!

Fang! Fang anything! Yes! That bit felt soft! That hurt it!

Roll again! Keep moving! It's got lots of tricks. It'll try to gas me again! Fang!

Yes! It let go. Run! Faster, it's catching me! Round here . . . Yes – it can't take corners as fast as me. But it's still right behind me!

I can smell poop! Wuzza! Follow the smell! It's close. Quick! Another corner.

It's a bit further behind, now. Aghhh! It shot out a cable-thing, trying to snare me! It's tricky.

Straight ahead – there's the poop-thing. I can't see any cleaner-toys around. That's good. Go for it. Go for it! Jump!

Yes! Made it! But here comes the metal-monster. It's stopped! It knows I can't run any further in here. It's got me.

Come on – come on. A few steps further. Yes. Now it's stopped in the doorway. Just looking at me with beady eyes. Stay there – stay there . . . Wait for it . . .

Bang! Wuzza!

The door's squashed him flat! Wuzza! It didn't see that coming. Clever Hobart! Now it's just like a broken toy of Glenn's. All in bits and pieces. Even Lincoln couldn't put him back together, now.

Wait – what's that? The box. The one with all the dog poop in it. It's moving. It's on tracks like Glenn's train set. It's rolling towards the doors on the other side of the room. The doors that lead out to the darkness and cold.

Will those doors open and let it out? I haven't seen this toy working before.

It's getting close to the door, now. It'll open for sure. I don't think this is a good idea. I don't think I'll like it when the doors open.

I don't believe it! I dropped my toy again!

It's stuck in the wheel thing with the gears and belts. Wait – the wheel's stopped turning!

The poop box has stopped!

Good toy. Stay there. Maybe those doors won't open, now. They're quiet. They're staying closed. That's good, I think.

But the door that squashed the monster isn't moving, either.

I'm stuck!

A warning light flashed on the console above Alice.

'Oh – the pest controller-bot has gone offline,' she said.

'These robots get glitches sometimes. Not like we humans. It'll come back online in a universal minute.'

'Look – another alarm,' Alice noted.

'It looks like the poop-pod has jammed and can't be ejected,' said Zeke.

'Then fix it,' said Alice firmly.

'Why me?'

'Two reasons. You are here to do every menial task on this ship.'

'And secondly?'

'I don't want to do it.'

Zeke wasn't happy with that answer. He slumped as he trudged off.

'Send a man to do a robot's job . . .' he muttered.

In the jail on asteroid Gavin, Gemma was putting her trophy (the photo of the Clarks with Hobart) into the satchel she always carried. She walked confidently towards the cell door.

'Give that back!' came a voice.

Gemma turned. She hadn't expected any resistance, after her vivid display of fighting skills. She was surprised to see Simone facing her.

'Gonna make me?' Gemma asked, smiling.

'Sure! Put 'em up, you little green alien!'

Simone assumed an unconvincing boxing stance – if only she'd watched more episodes of *Planet Man*.

'You're an amateur,' said Gemma, confidently.

'True – but you're going down,' snarled Simone.

'It will take more than you,' said Gemma.

'Well, what about me?' said Gran, taking a stand next to Simone and adopting the same pose.

'And me,' said Lincoln, stepping up as well.

The three of them looked very determined, despite not having a shred of fighting credibility. Gemma seemed genuinely puzzled.

'Excuse me?' she queried. 'You realize you're in for a beating . . . ?'

The others nodded.

'You saw how easily I defeated your leader?'

The others nodded again, but didn't take a backward step.

'You realize I'm a formidable warrior, but you still wish to challenge me? Is this picture really that important to you?'

'Hobart is our pet. And our friend,' said Gran. 'Don't you understand about pets?'

'Animals are to eat, that's all,' said Gemma. And with that, she stepped out of the cell, closing the door behind her. Lincoln, Simone and Gran felt a bit silly in their fighting poses, now. They relaxed a little as Gemma observed them through the bars. She was trying to work them out.

'You're a strange race,' said Gemma, and she turned and started to leave the jail.

'Hey!' called Simone. 'Where are you going?'

'I can't fight you now. Tonight there is a big feast. We're having something special for dinner.'

Lincoln frowned. He didn't like the sound of that. 'How do you mean "special"?' he asked.

'It's a brand-new kind of pink food,' Gemma replied. 'We found it on your ship.'

'Oh no! My masterpiece!' cried Lincoln.

'What do you call this pink, furry thing?'

'His name is Boombah!' yelled Simone. 'And you can't eat him.'

'Why not?'

'Because I'll never be able to make another one,' sighed Lincoln. 'And without him, we can't locate the *Dogstar*!'

'You made him?' asked Gemma, quite puzzled.

'It's hard to explain, but he's very rare.'

'Don't worry,' said Gemma, walking out the door cheerfully. 'We'll cook him so he's *medium* rare!'

The door slammed behind her and Lincoln, Simone and Gran exchanged worried looks. Suddenly, Glenn sat up.

'Is it safe to get up now?' he asked.

'Yes it is, but we've got to save Boombah,' Lincoln declared.

'But there are hundreds of those Gavinians out there,' said Simone. 'They may not be a very advanced race . . .'

'Their only weapon seems to be the rock,' observed Gran.

'Exactly,' said Simone, 'but there're a lot more of them than there are of us.'

'Hopeless odds don't worry me,' said Glenn from where he stood examining the lock on the cell door.

'Then again, you've been hit on the head a lot lately.'

'You won't be laughing at me when I pick the lock to this door,' said Glenn.

Glenn opened the front of his Vacuum Suit, removed the belt from the trousers he was wearing underneath, and inserted the pointy bit into the lock.

'Since when do you know how to pick locks?' Simone asked.

'Since I saw Planet Man do it in Episode 241. When he was imprisoned by the evil Sessionoids, he picked the lock to his cell using only his belt buckle.'

Lincoln sighed. 'That seems highly unlikely . . .'

But suddenly, as Glenn pressed against it, the door to the cell opened.

'Ohhhh . . .' said Glenn.

'You did it!' gasped Simone. 'I hate to admit it, but I'm impressed. What now?'

Lincoln stepped forward. His brain was working rapidly.

'I have a plan,' he said. 'Gran and I will go back and fix the bubble wrap on the *Valiant* to facilitate our escape. You two must go and rescue Boombah.'

'Interesting, interesting,' said Glenn. 'Why don't we fix the bubble wrap and you two rescue Boombah?'

'It's simple,' said Lincoln. 'You two are better runners. If there's a chase, you two have the best chance of success.'

'So true, so true,' said Glenn. 'I *am* the best runner in the family.'

'After me,' said Simone.

'As if!'

'It's true!'

'Please!' cried Lincoln, interrupting. 'Boombah may not have much time!'

Simone and Glenn stopped bickering. They nodded solemnly.

Seven minutes later, Glenn and Simone were creeping through the Gavinian village. Actually, it was barely a village. There were a few rough huts made from piling rocks on top of one another. It was all pretty basic.

They crawled along a low rock wall towards the sound of distant chanting. As they got closer, Simone got more nervous.

'Who are we kidding?' she whispered. 'We won't be able to snatch Boombah from under their noses. We don't have a *real* rescue plan.'

'Heroes *act*, Simone,' said Glenn. 'They don't think, they don't plan, they just *do*! Now be quiet.'

They were close to the chanting sound. They peered out from behind some rocks to see a ghastly spectacle. Boombah was tied to a spit over a fire-pit. The fire wasn't lit yet, but the Gavinian Chef (you could tell from the hat) was basting Boombah with mysterious herbs and spices. It actually smelt rather appetizing. A ceremonial priest-figure was presiding over the special occasion, leading the chant.

Circled round the fire-pit were about a hundred wide-eyed Gavinians. They stared hungrily at the meal in front of them as they chanted. Glenn tried to pick Gemma out in the crowd, but all the Gavinians looked pretty much the same to him.

'There – see?' said Simone. 'No chance.'

'I have a plan,' said Glenn, suddenly. 'You're going to run out there and create a diversion. While the aliens are throwing rocks at you, I'll sneak in there and untie Boombah.'

'That's the stupidest thing I've ever heard of!'

'It worked for Planet Man when he asked his trusty side-kick Solar Lad to do it.'

'And what happened to Solar Lad?'

'I never really found out,' said Glenn. 'In the next episode he'd been replaced by Meteor Boy.'

'Think of something else,' said Simone.

Glenn was silent.

So was Simone.

It was only then that they realized that the Gavinians had gone silent too. Simone and Glenn looked out again.

All the Gavinians were standing still. Their eyes were closed and their heads faced downwards. It was as if they were meditating – or offering up a prayer.

'It seems to be part of the ceremony,' whispered Glenn. 'They're probably giving thanks to their deity for the feast.'

'That's good enough for me. Let's go!'

Without consultation, or analysis, or reasoned debate, Simone stood up suddenly. She started sneaking towards Boombah. Another impulsive act! Glenn could hardly believe it. Normally, Simone would have been happy to argue strategy for another hour at least – but here she was, halfway to Boombah! Glenn had no choice but to follow.

Glenn and Simone moved as silently as they possibly could. It helped that the area was very dusty. Their footsteps made no sound at all. They slowly crept closer and closer.

At the *Valiant*, Lincoln was busily reattaching bubble wrap to the hull. It wasn't easy, and his concentration was being affected by the popping sounds in the background.

'Would you mind not doing that, Gran?' he asked.

Gran had been sitting, popping bubble-wrap bubbles.

'Sorry, Lincoln,' she sighed. 'Let me help you.'

At the fire-pit, Glenn was starting to sweat. He had untied Boombah's front paws from the spit. Simone supported the feline while Glenn untied the back legs. Just as he removed the knot, Boombah's eyes opened. It was hard to believe – up until now he'd been asleep! He yawned and looked at Glenn and Simone.

They quickly put their fingers to their lips to shoosh him, but cats aren't known for their ability to read sign language.

Boombah miaowed.

Glenn and Simone froze. They looked around. The Gavinians' eyes were still closed. All, that is, except the chef's!

'Hey!' he cried, and pointed at the interlopers. 'Sacrilege! Grab them!'

Instantly, all the Gavinians opened their eyes! Glenn and Simone took off, carrying Boombah between them. The Gavinians gave chase, pausing only to pick up rocks and throw them.

It was immediately apparent that Simone was the faster runner. She grabbed Boombah on her own and outpaced Glenn. In his Vacuum Suit, Glenn struggled to keep up, but this had a hidden benefit.

He was between Simone and the rock-pelting Gavinians. The Gavinians were still deadly accurate with their throws. Rocks rebounded off Glenn's suit without really hurting him, so they targeted his helmet. Stone after stone bounced off it.

'Are you all right?' Simone called back as she ran.

'Yes! Keep going!' yelled Glenn. His ears were ringing as rocks made his helmet reverberate.

Gran was just replacing the last of the bubble wrap when she and Lincoln heard the frightful sounds. They looked up.

Simone was running towards them as fast as she could, still carrying Boombah. Behind her was Glenn, and behind Glenn were a hundred screaming Gavinians – throwing rocks and running hard.

'Start the engines!' yelled Simone as she got closer.

Lincoln and Gran raced into the ship.

As Simone jumped aboard, the engines began warming up. Simone paused in the doorway, waiting for Glenn.

'Come on!' she yelled back to him.

With one last lunge, Glenn leapt aboard and the hatch slammed behind him. He could hear the drumming of rocks on the bubble-wrapped hull. They were safe at last.

The *Valiant* shot into the air leaving the Gavinians to lament their lost feast. They released their frustrations by throwing rocks at other, larger rocks.

It was all they could think of.

The *BobCat* sat doing absolutely nothing in a very boring location at the edge of the asteroid field, and Bob Santino was getting slightly testy.

'Status report, Daina,' he shouted suddenly, breaking the silence.

'Instruments show no signs of movement within the asteroid field. No other life forms nearby – and no other spacecraft in the immediate vicinity.'

Santino said nothing.

Perhaps the only trait Bob and Dino Santino had in common was their mutual dislike of silence. Dino watched the strained expression on his father's face as they sat still, no one speaking. The tension was palpable – to Dino at least.

'That was a very thorough report, Daina,' said Dino suddenly. 'Wasn't it, Father? Wasn't it a thorough report? Detailed. Comprehensive without being too wordy.'

'Dino . . . ?'

'Yes, Father?'

'You're not helping.'

'Yes, Father.'

•

'Great take-off, Gran,' said Glenn.

'It reminds me of those glory days with Billy Picken's Aerobatic Squadron!' she chirped. Glenn and Simone exchanged a worried look. Glenn resolved to slip out of the Vacuum Suit and take over the controls as soon as possible.

The *Valiant* glided through what little atmosphere Gavin possessed and soared back into the teeth of the asteroid field. In her best imitation of Glenn's flying style, Gran skipped round the larger obstacles. Some of the smaller chunks collided with the ship, but the bubble wrap held firm. The concussions to the hull were a little disturbing to those inside, but Simone started up a conversation to break the tension.

'Thank heavens they didn't eat Boombah,' she said.

'Yes,' relayed Lincoln, somewhat forlornly. 'We're free to continue our mission to find the *Dogstar*.'

'Something bothering you, Lincoln?'

'I . . . I just wish we hadn't lost the picture of Hobart. I . . . really feel its absence greatly.'

'I agree,' sighed Simone. 'I don't like to think of it in the hands of that irritating little brat.'

'Who are you calling a brat?'

Lincoln and Simone jumped as they heard the voice. Gran didn't jump so much as twitch – the bionics in her legs were only so good. It was Gemma, the Gavinian.

As she emerged from her hiding place, Lincoln and Simone took a wary step back.

'What are you doing here?' asked Gran.

'I'm a stowaway,' Gemma replied.

'That doesn't answer the question,' was Lincoln's canny observation.

Slowly, Gemma reached into her satchel. The Clarks expected the worst, but Gemma simply removed the photo of Hobart and the family. She looked at it for a moment, then spoke. 'Can I help you find this Hobart?'

It was at this moment that Glenn returned to the bridge minus his Vacuum Suit, just in time to hear Gemma's suggestion.

'Hey! You! You can't be in here!' he yelled.

Gemma looked him up and down.

'And you've shrunk,' she noted.

Lincoln stepped forward. He reached out a hand for the photo. Gemma hesitated for a moment, then handed it to him. Lincoln clutched it tightly.

'Check that it isn't booby-trapped,' muttered Glenn as he glanced across at Gran flying the ship. He always got nervous when she had the controls for more than three minutes.

'I admit, I'm curious,' said Gemma. 'This Hobart means so much to you that you're willing to risk your lives. I would like to find out why.'

'Absolutely not!' said Simone. 'She's not coming!'

'Listen, Simone,' said Glenn, half-listening, half-watching Gran. 'As honorary leader, I should decide.'

'Since when were you honorary leader?'

'Since I picked the lock of that prison cell. Remember? All you managed to do was tell a bunch of aliens to sit on a cactus.'

Simone folded her arms and fumed. Glenn walked over

to Gemma and glared at her.

'Give me one good reason why I should trust you,' he said.

'I helped you escape,' whispered Gemma.

'How?'

'I left the prison door unlocked.'

'Ohhh . . . right,' whispered Glenn. 'I'd really appreciate it if you didn't tell the others.'

'Sure. I understand.'

'Excuse me,' came Lincoln's voice. 'We have a problem.'

Gemma and Glenn turned to Lincoln. He was facing the view-screen. Gran had successfully negotiated a path through the asteroid field. The way ahead was getting clearer. But outside the asteroid field, one obstacle still remained.

The *BobCat* was waiting for them.

When audio alarms on the bridge suddenly sounded, Bob and Dino Santino nearly leapt out of their skin. Dino had been preoccupied with creative drawing and Bob had started to nod off.

'Aha!' was their combined reaction.

Daina, however, was ice-cold. Constantly vigilant, the news that instruments had detected a small craft approaching from the centre of the asteroid field neither surprised nor excited her.

She simply responded efficiently and activated every weapon system on the ship.

Zeke entered the Poop Pod Bay on D-Deck and immediately saw the remains of the mangled pest-exterminator-bot squashed in the inner air-lock door.

'Silly pest-controller-bot,' he sighed.

The inner door closed behind him and he surveyed the room. The Poop Pod was approaching the end of its track. It had stopped just before the outer door for some reason. What he didn't see was Hobart, hiding in the shadows on the other side of the room. He had hidden himself when he heard the inner door opening. Zeke pressed a button on the intercom device near the door. Alice's face appeared on the screen.

'I'm down here, Alice,' said Zeke.

'So what's causing the malfunction?'

'I don't know, Alice. The pest-controller-bot managed to get himself squashed by the inner door. Would that be the problem?'

'No, it's incidental information. You should only call me when you've assessed the problem with the Poop Pod. If you find a way to fix it, do so. If you feel the need to get a second opinion at that time, it would be appropriate to talk to me then.'

Zeke paused. 'You know, Alice? I think this is proof I'm human. You're actually annoying me.'

The screen suddenly went dark. Alice had hung up on him. Zeke shrugged and turned to the task. He walked over to the gearing mechanism and immediately saw the problem.

'That's funny. How did that get there?'

He reached down into the mechanism and, not without effort, pulled Hobart's chewable toy from the gears. Freed up again, they immediately started whirring.

The Poop Pod moved once more, slowly heading towards the outer door. Zeke pressed the button to open the inner door.

Nothing happened.

He frowned and pressed it again.

Again, nothing.

Zeke was feeling a little concerned now. He looked towards the Poop Pod. It was still moving towards the outer door. When it reached the end of the rails, the outer hatch would open into space. The Poop Pod would be ejected into the vacuum. Zeke pressed the button on the intercom.

'Alice? Alice? The inner door isn't opening.'

'That's right, Zeke,' said Alice whose face now appeared on the screen. If robots could smile, she would have been grinning. 'I've locked it from here.'

'You what? You can't do that.'

'I think you'll find I have, Zeke. That's why you can't open the door.'

'But the moment the outer hatch opens, I'll be sucked into space! It's a vacuum, Alice! I'll die!'

'See, Zeke, here's where we think differently. You're a robot, Zeke – not a human. When the outer hatch opens, nothing will happen to you. You'll be fine.'

'Stop mucking around! Open the Pod Bay door, Al–'

'I'm afraid I can't do that, Zeke.'

Zeke tried to think of a reply, but he couldn't. He tried to think of a way out – there was none. So Zeke took a moment to reflect. Then he sat down.

I don't like that. It's got my toy. I should get it back, but I still don't trust the big-doll. I'll stay here where it can't see me. Maybe it'll drop it.

Why did it start the machine again? It's moving towards the door again. I have a bad feeling.

The big-doll is sitting down. It talked to the other one and now it looks sad. It's just sitting and staring at that door. It reminds me of Mark. Just sitting there. Staring. Like it's waiting for something bad to arrive.

Should I talk to it? If it doesn't want the doors to open, either, why doesn't it just use my toy again? Maybe it's not very clever. What to do . . .?

It's dropped my toy, now. It's thrown it over its shoulder like it doesn't care about it any more. Should I . . .? Okay – here I go. I'll try. Quiet, Hobart . . . quiet.

There. I've got my toy and it didn't even notice. Sneaky Hobart. Good dog. I'll put it back in those wheels. Here goes . . . There.

It's slowing up. Yes! The gears have stopped again. My toy has jammed them up. I think that's a good thing. I hope that's a good thing. Now maybe I can go back to my hiding spot before it . . .

Uh oh . . . it's seen me.

If Zeke was genuinely human, his jaw would've metaphorically dropped when it saw Hobart there with him in the Poop Pod Bay. As it was, his processors missed a beat.

'What are you doing here?' he asked Hobart.

Hobart just stood still.

'You're meant to be with the other dogs.'

Hobart didn't move. Zeke thought he looked a little scared.

'You shouldn't be in this bay,' said Zeke sternly. 'It's a very dangerous place. If that outer door opens, you'll be . . .'

Zeke stopped. Reality suddenly hit him in his motherboard. He punched the intercom button.

'Alice! Alice! Look! There's a dog in here!'

Alice appeared on screen looking a little miffed. 'That was very clever of you to jam the Poop Pod, Zeke, but I'm not opening the door till you admit you're not a human!'

'Alice! Look! Even if I don't die in the vacuum of space, this dog will!'

This new information forced Alice to think for a moment.

'And remember, Alice,' pleaded Zeke, 'our primary mission instructions state that we're to deliver all the dogs safely to New Earth. Am I right, or not?'

'I hadn't thought of that,' said Alice, finally.

For a long moment, Alice was frozen on the screen – deep in thought.

'You're right,' said Alice reluctantly. 'That is our prime directive.'

'Thank you, Alice,' Zeke sighed as the inner door opened.

'But you're still a robot!' Alice called before shutting off the intercom once more.

As the inner door opened, Hobart looked at it as if he thought he should run, then he sniffed the air. His toy was still here. He wagged his tail as Zeke walked over and removed the toy from the gears.

The Poop Pod started again, slowly trundling towards the end of its track. Now a warning light started to flash on the outer door. Zeke scooped up Hobart and walked quickly to the inner door.

'Hurry, dog, we don't want to be sucked out.'

But as Zeke stepped through the door, he casually dropped the toy. The inner door slammed shut with Hobart and Zeke safe, but the chewable toy wasn't with them.

When Zeke put him down, Hobart ran straight back to the closed door. It seemed to Zeke that Hobart had a strange expression as he stared through the view-port. The outer hatch opened and the large Poop Pod shot out into space, but Zeke noticed that Hobart had his eyes firmly fixed on a smaller object floating out with it. Hobart's toy.

'Oh . . .' said Zeke. 'Did you want that?'

Hobart whimpered just a little as the toy was lost from view.

'Sorry . . .'

Why did it do that? Why did it throw away my toy?

Now it's put me on a lead. Where did that come from? Where's it taking me?

This is bad. I try to pull away, but it's too strong. I don't know where we're going, but I bet it isn't good.

Oh no – now I see. The big-doll is taking me to the funny part of the kennel. The place I don't like. Right up the front. But why? Have I been a bad dog?

What's it going to do to me?

Do big-dolls eat dogs?

A photon bolt exploded next to the *Valiant*, frying the bubble wrap that remained on it. It sparkled with blue and yellow flame, briefly, but only lightly scorched the hull of the *Valiant*.

Glenn was now behind the controls and trying desperately to stay away from the *BobCat*'s weapons.

'Who is in that ship shooting at us?' asked Gemma.

'Our mortal enemy,' said Lincoln.

None of the Clarks noticed the steely gleam in Gemma's eye as she watched the *BobCat* on the screen. It wasn't exactly a pretty sight.

Daina was throwing everything at them. Glenn dodged to starboard and almost ran into a burst of laser cannon. He dived to port, but had to evade two missiles. No matter what Glenn did, the *BobCat* was getting closer each second. Every turn Glenn made was matched by the *BobCat*. The best computers money can buy had a tracking lock on the *Valiant* and they weren't going to lose the enemy again.

'Why aren't you throwing things at it?' demanded Gemma. 'If your enemy throws, you throw – they're the rules!'

'We don't have anything to throw!' Simone yelled back at her.

Aboard the *BobCat*, Santino laughed. 'Well, it looks like the bad guys win after all. Immobilize at will, Daina!'

'Can I say that, Father?' said Dino.

'Oh . . . all right, Dino.'

Dino tried to get his voice sounding as deep as possible. 'Immobilize at will, Daina,' he said – but alas it came out squeaky and ineffectual.

'It didn't quite have it, did it, Father?'

Aboard the *Valiant*, every one of the Clarks could see the end coming rather more quickly than they'd like. As the *BobCat* got bigger and bigger on their view-screen, they knew it was only a matter of time.

Boombah was highly agitated. Unusually for this less-than-athletic feline, he'd begun to claw at a chair on the bridge and hiss at the air.

'He's scared,' said Simone, and grabbed him. She dropped him into the portal leading to the nose-cone. The vacuum tube quickly deposited Boombah back into his familiar domain as more missiles shot past the fleeing *Valiant*. The Clarks were thrown around helplessly as the ship veered left – then right.

'Incoming object directly ahead,' yelled Lincoln as a photon bolt hit somewhere near the rear of the *Valiant*.

He turned off the damage-warning alarm, the puling of which was making him feel nauseous. The *Valiant* was sounding different. Whatever the photon bolt hit was important. The ship's speed slowed a little.

'Incoming!' yelled Lincoln again.

'Ahead of us? Is it a missile?' asked Glenn, still desperately trying to shake the *BobCat*.

Lincoln brought the object up on the screen.

Unnoticed by all of them, Boombah was going ballistic in his nose-cone. He was clawing at the glass and growling like a caged lion – albeit a round, pink, fluffy one.

More important, however, was the object on the main screen – a huge, metallic, box-like object coming straight for them.

'I'm not sure what it is,' said Lincoln, a note of desperation in his voice.

'Is it one of their weapons?' yelled Glenn.

'No!' said Gemma suddenly. 'But it could become one of ours! Hold your course!'

Gemma had leapt up to stand right behind Glenn. Her tail slapped the hand that Glenn was pulling back on the controls with. Her eyes were alive as she watched the object getting bigger on the screen. She was actually enjoying this.

'We'll hit it!' said Glenn as a missile just missed on the port side.

'Hold your course!' repeated Gemma. There was something in her voice you didn't want to argue with. 'A good warrior doesn't show all his weapons to the enemy. He keeps his best stone till last.'

'Is that a Planet Man quote?'

'Who?'

'Doesn't matter.'

Glenn held his course, but the incoming object was now almost filling the view-screen.

'Ten seconds to impact,' said Lincoln coolly.

'Minor hull breaches in Cargo Hold Four – but I'm sealing it off,' said Simone, pushing buttons frantically.

'I've re-routed life-support power to the engines,' said Gran. 'We've slowed, but this'll keep you ahead of Santino for . . .'

'Impact in three seconds.'

'Turn now!' yelled Gemma, and Glenn immediately jerked on the controls. He pulled straight up and the object passed just under the *Valiant*.

The *BobCat*, unsighted by the *Valiant* and right on its tail, had no chance to avoid it.

The Poop Pod from the *Dogstar*, travelling at over a million miles an hour, hit the *BobCat* hard, smashing headlong into the cockpit.

Seven tonnes of canine faecal matter exploded like a brown-and-ochre-toned fireworks display. The *BobCat* was instantly covered with . . . well . . . Anyone familiar with twentieth-century painter Jackson Pollock will be aware of his splatter paintings. Bright. Colourful. Vibrant. But no artist could possibly imagine the sheer revulsion this particular splatter evoked.

Saint Bernard poop is quite large. A Mexican Hairless's poop, by contrast, is relatively small. A Beagle's can be soft or hard depending on its diet. Even a vegetarian Irish Wolfhound's poop is not a pretty sight – it can have yellowish tints. But the explosive combination of every shade, colour and texture of all types of dog poop all at once is something that sets whole new standards of revolting grossness. Such an event was happening now.

'The instruments are all out, sir!' cried Daina. 'We've lost visibility! Nothing is working!'

'What was that?' said Santino. 'I thought they didn't have any weapons? And why has the view gone that browny colour?'

Daina was too busy to reply, bringing the ship to a complete stop before they ran into anything else.

Dino was looking at the ominous cracks in the supposedly unbreakable glass surrounds of the cockpit.

'What's that funny smell?' he said. 'It seems to be getting stronger.'

Aboard the *Valiant*, Simone and Lincoln checked instruments frantically.

'Life support at ninety-two per cent.'

'Pressure stabilizing.'

'Sealing cargo-holds three to nine.'

'Spray-epoxy hull patches activated.'

'Are we okay?'

'Everything seems to be satisfactory,' said Lincoln.

'Where's Santino?' asked Simone.

Glenn pushed a few buttons and the *BobCat* appeared on screen. It was stationary and almost unrecognizable – just a large, putrid, brown blob.

'That was fantastic, Gemma!' said Glenn. 'It reminded me a lot of Planet Man. Sharp on tactics. Cool in a crisis.'

'Who is he talking about?' Gemma asked Lincoln.

'It doesn't matter,' replied Lincoln. 'The thing is, your tactical creativity has resulted in a resounding victory against our greatest adversary.'

'Of course,' said Gemma. 'You need a warrior on your team. No offence, but . . . I think I can make a difference.'

The Clarks exchanged glances. Should they? Or shouldn't they?

Simone nodded.

Gran smiled.

Glenn thought for a moment, but gave a thumbs up.

Lincoln, always inscrutable, turned back to Gemma. 'The consensus would indicate you've been accepted into our crew,' he said. 'Can I say that personally I support the decision.'

'Excellent!' cried Gemma. 'I give you – the Gavinian oath of allegiance!'

With that, Gemma quickly whipped off her left boot. Before anyone could say anything, she put her big toe in her mouth and bit it off!

The Clarks were aghast as she swallowed it.

'Urrggghh,' was the collective response.

Gemma was smiling, however. Before their eyes, the toe began growing back on her foot. In mere seconds it was as good as new.

'Impressive,' said Glenn.

Lincoln surveyed the bridge. Warning lights were still flashing, a few sparks came from damaged controls, but the ship was secure and the future was looking a lot better than five minutes ago.

Then a different screen caught his attention.

On the B-Cam monitor, Boombah was going crazy. In the confines of the nose-cone, he was leaping around clawing at everything he could find. Every surface had scratch marks on it. His puffy cushion was shredded.

'Funny . . . Boombah's still agitated . . .' muttered Lincoln as he casually switched on the audio channel.

Suddenly, everyone clamped their hands over their ears as a piercing shriek filled the control room.

'Are we being attacked again?' yelled Glenn.

'It's Boombah,' said Lincoln, hastily shutting off the sound. The Clarks stared aghast at the sight of Boombah clawing at his glass cage.

'Battle fatigue,' said Glenn solemnly. 'I've seen it before in an episode of . . .'

'He smells dogs!' cried Lincoln.

'Are you sure?'

'Yes. Look at him. Agitated. Sweating. They're the symptoms. But how? What's he looking at?'

Lincoln pressed more buttons on his controls. He made calculations – measuring angles based on Boombah's line of sight and the direction of his claw marks. On the main screen, the cameras zeroed in on the *BobCat*.

'The *BobCat?*' asked Glenn. 'There are no dogs there.'

'Unless . . .' Lincoln made the camera's zoom-lens zero in closer still, ignoring the involuntary regurgitation reflex in his throat as he examined the turgid spectacle. 'The instruments are analysing that strange, brown matter,' he noted. 'It seems to be . . .'

'What?'

'As impossible as it seems, the substance that rendered the *BobCat* inoperative is canine faecal excretion.'

'Pardon?' said Glenn.

'Dog poop!' shouted Gran.

'Exactly,' said Lincoln. 'But where in the universe could dog poop possibly originate, unless . . .'

The camera zoomed in even closer on to the putrid spectacle. Each of the Clarks fought back rising waves of nausea. The camera settled on some shards of metal that had burst like shrapnel, embedding themselves in the hull of the *BobCat*. On one of the shards was a small logo and the words 'PROPERTY OF DOGSTAR'.

'The *Dogstar*?' queried Glenn.

'It's a Poop Pod from the *Dogstar*!' shouted Simone.

'Is that good?' asked Gemma.

'It's very good,' said Lincoln, thinking fast. 'The Poop Pod's initial flight trajectory will be recorded in the database.' Lincoln was frantically pushing buttons as he spoke. 'I'm retrieving it now. By following that trajectory we'll surely find its point of origin!'

'You mean the *Dogstar*?' asked Gran.

'That's exactly what I mean!' shouted Lincoln.

On the screen, a set of numbers and charts appeared. The Poop Pod's path was clearly visible, ending with its impact on the *BobCat*. Navigation coordinates followed – a series of hypothetical flight paths intersecting at a distant point in space.

'I get it!' cried Glenn and hit the thrusters. 'Hold on!'

The *Valiant* made the jump to hyperspace and vanished from this quadrant of the universe.

Right about now, back on New Earth, it was a warmish night in the suburb where the Clark house stood. Mark Clark was sitting in his pyjamas on the front doorstep, looking up at the night sky. Mark wasn't the type to lose himself in solitary thought very often, but this was one of those times.

'What are you doing out here?'

Mark turned and found Greta behind him. He sighed. Then he pointed up at the stars twinkling above.

'Look,' he mused. 'The stars. It's the one thing I can't get used to here on New Earth. You can actually see them.'

'They're beautiful,' sighed Greta, sitting down with him on the step.

'They just go on and on forever,' muttered Mark. 'You forget just how big it is out there. Millions of galaxies – billions of stars. And it's expanding, Greta – you know that, right?'

Greta put her arm around Mark and smiled at him. 'You're worried about them, aren't you?' she said.

'Of course. I've always thought it was a one-in-a-million chance that I ever found you, Greta. How can the kids possibly find Hobart in all that . . . ?'

He gestured upwards vaguely.

'There's nothing you can do about it, Mark.'

'I know, I know . . .'

'And think about it – you managed to find me, why can't they find Hobart?'

Mark thought about this. He sighed.

'Maybe you're right, Greta. Maybe I should trust them more. Or maybe some things are just fate.'

'Maybe. Are you coming inside?' asked Greta, standing.

'I might just sit out here for a while.'

'I'll make you a nice veal-substitute sandwich with pseudo-bread and reconstituted lettuce.'

'Yeah – okay,' said Mark, and followed her indoors.

The journey from D-Deck up to the *Dogstar* bridge takes around seven minutes. You take three separate lifts and two travelators. For every step of the journey, Zeke kept looking down at the dog he was leading.

'How did you get out?' he asked, as if Hobart could answer. Zeke shook his head.

On A-Deck, they came across a squad of tiny cleaner-bots carrying some unidentified waste material to a receptacle.

Upon seeing Hobart, the cleaner-bots scattered and ran away. Clearly, word of the pest-exterminator-bot's demise had spread among them. Zeke was confused by the expression on Hobart's face. He looked almost proud.

'What's his name?' asked Alice after Zeke had explained Hobart's presence in the control room of the *Dogstar*.

Zeke checked the name tag. 'Hobart,' he said.

'Rroowwff!' said Hobart, recognizing his name.

'He's saying hello,' said Alice. 'Hello, Hobart.'

'Wwrroof!' replied Hobart.

'He seems very clever, Alice,' said Zeke. 'I like him. Maybe he could stay up here with us?'

'That would be against the rules, Zeke. You know that.'

'That's true, Alice. But who is going to know?'

Alice thought about this.

'Is this some strange attempt to prove you're human, Zeke? That "humans have pets", therefore . . .?'

'No. No. No, Alice. I simply . . . like Hobart.'

Alice looked down at Hobart. Hobart wagged his tail.

'I like him, too,' she said. 'All right, he can stay.'

The one called Zeke is ruffing me on my head! Yes! I like that!

The one called Alice is ruffing me, too! Wuzza!

That's what I've been missing! Ruffs! This feels good! Perhaps these big-dolls aren't so bad after all. Hahahaaa . . . Zeke is rubbing my tummy when I roll over. That's it. That's it . . . Hahahaa.

It's funny in this big kennel. Are those two a pack? They sure argue like one.

That reminds me . . .

Mark, Greta, Gran, Simone, Glenn and Lincoln.
Mark, Greta, Gran, Simone, Glenn and Lincoln.
Mark, Greta, Gran, Simone, Glenn and Lincoln.

The *Valiant* emerged from the jump with a flash and decelerated as it entered normal space. Its hull was clearly scarred by the hits it had taken from Santino's weaponry. Parts were scorched by the near-misses, but it was still capable of a short hyperspace jump and its crew were grateful for that. Santino couldn't follow them now, even if he had a working spaceship.

On the bridge, Lincoln was absorbed in calculations. Charts and graphs were all over the main screen.

'Observe,' he said. 'I calculate that the Poop Pod originated at a point close to here.'

The position was immediately illuminated on the screen.

'Allowing for the solar wind-drag and the gravitational pull of every celestial body along its flight path, I've calculated that the Poop Pod was ejected while the *Dogstar* was travelling at its sub-light maximum speed.'

'How did you work that out?' asked Gemma.

'I used my brain.'

'Fair enough,' said Glenn.

'The *Dogstar* was therefore travelling away from this point, here – on *this* heading . . .'

A new set of figures appeared on screen. A red line cut through the star charts – the *Dogstar*'s flight path.

'If we follow this heading, we find the *Dogstar*.'

'But it could have changed course,' cried Simone.

'Perhaps – but there is one other factor I've used in calculating this heading. Observe . . .'

The B-Cam picture of Boombah flashed up on the main screen. Boombah, now thoroughly exhausted and barely able to move, was clawing pathetically at the window. His eyes were fixed into the distance. He was staring at exactly the heading indicated by Lincoln. He was miaowing weakly.

'Follow that flight path,' commanded Lincoln.

'Can do!' cried Glenn.

The *Valiant* leapt forward. Its engines had been slightly affected by fire from the *BobCat*. As it moved off, there was a shudder in the superstructure.

'No!' said Simone. 'Don't give up on us now!'

But the *Valiant* surged forward, engines coughing occasionally.

'Does it always sound this bad?' asked Gemma.

'The engines are only working at seventy-eight per cent effectiveness,' replied Lincoln. 'I hope it's enough.'

'But this ship can't compete with the *Dogstar*'s top speed,' said Glenn, quite correctly.

'I'm hoping it doesn't always travel at that speed.'

'Hoping?' asked Gran.

'Hoping,' replied Lincoln. 'We can hope, can't we?'

There was silence in the control room. Unscientific words like 'hope' didn't usually come from Lincoln. That's how bad things were. Each of the Clark family members closed their eyes. Each of them in their own way allowed themselves some hope.

Watching them, Gemma was silent.

•

'Should we make a jump?' asked Alice.

'Why do you want to make a jump, Alice?'

'Wherever we are, we're lost. Perhaps jumping to a new quadrant will bring us into contact with familiar star fields.'

'Perhaps you're right, Alice.'

'Wrroff!' said Hobart, for no particular reason.

'What's that, Hobart?' asked Zeke. 'Do you think we should make the jump?'

'Wrroaaww,' replied Hobart as Zeke scratched his ears.

'I don't think Hobart agrees,' said Zeke.

'Can you speak canine now, Zeke? Are you a dog now? Is that it?'

'Hobart might be right, Alice. A random jump could take us further away from our destination.'

'Or closer.'

'But it's a gamble.'

'You'd prefer to do nothing?'

'Maybe.'

'That's silly.'

'Is it, Alice? Maybe we've been going about this all wrong?'

'How do you mean?'

'Well – we're the ones who got lost. We've tried many different things and we still can't find our way to New Earth. Maybe everything we've chosen to do is wrong.'

Alice thought about this.

'For the sake of argument,' she said, 'let's assume you are correct. What is the alternative, Zeke? If we do the opposite, we're *choosing* to do that. It's still *our* choice. There's no way around that.'

'There is one way.'

'What's that?'

Zeke looked at Hobart decisively. 'Let Hobart choose.'

'Hobart?'

Alice looked at Hobart. His tail was wagging as Zeke patted him. 'Very well, Zeke. Why not? It's not as if we could do any worse.'

Zeke jumped up with excitement. 'Good choice, Alice!' he said. He turned to Hobart and adopted a very serious tone. 'Hobart?' he asked. 'What should we do?'

Hobart stared at them both for a moment.

Don't stop! I was enjoying the ruffing! Ruffing's the best. Come on! More! More!

Why are they looking at me like that? I've got no idea. Come on – do the big-dolls need me to show them how to do everything?

At that exact moment, Hobart rolled over on to his back and put his legs in the air. Hobart's intention was, naturally enough, 'scratch my tummy'. Zeke and Alice, of course, saw it very differently. They turned to each other.

'I see,' said Zeke.

'Do you think we should?' asked Alice.

'We agreed to do whatever Hobart decided, Alice.'

'But . . . to just stop still . . .?'

'In a way, it makes sense. We've been searching everywhere without any luck. If we just stop, maybe someone will come and find us.'

Alice shrugged. 'All right. I'm happy to try.'

And with that, Alice turned off the giant plasma engines. The dull throbbing that always permeated the Space Ark was instantly silenced. Throughout the ship, dogs everywhere stood and listened. Something was different, but they had no idea what. A firing of stabilizing jets brought the ship to a complete standstill.

The *Dogstar* hung there in space. Silent.

Waiting.

'See anything?' asked Simone. She was watching Lincoln's face as he scoured endless streams of data from his instruments. Glenn steered the ship on a straight course but had one eye on his instruments, too. He didn't like what he was seeing.

'Losing power in the number-two engine,' he noted. 'We took a few hits back there from Santino. I'll have to slow up a little.'

'But what about the *Dogstar*?' cried Simone.

'If I keep pushing both the engines at maximum power, they could overheat and shut down.'

'Glenny's right,' said Gran. 'We don't want to be marooned in space like your uncle Ross. When they found him he was like a baked potato.'

Glenn eased back on the power a little.

Suddenly, an explosion rocked the ship. It came from the rear. Warning lights blinked and alarms sounded.

'Is it Santino?' asked Gran.

'It's engine number two,' yelled Glenn. 'Plasma surge. I'm shutting it down!'

Glenn adjusted the relevant controls. The vibrations

racking the ship diminished. Lincoln turned off the piercing alarm sounds, but the warning lights remained flashing. Gemma was hanging by her tail from a pipe above Glenn's pilot seat. She frowned.

'Is everything all right?' she asked.

'No, it's not!' Glenn sighed. 'That's it. We've lost the number-two engine.'

'Total engine power is now only at forty-two per cent,' reported Lincoln.

'How are we supposed to catch the *Dogstar* now?' cried Gran.

'We have to keep trying,' said Simone.

'I am trying, Simone,' said Glenn glumly. 'But our chances of catching it just plummeted. Right, Lincoln?'

Lincoln said nothing. Of course, Glenn was statistically right, but Lincoln was hoping other, unknowable factors were at play.

There was silence in the *Valiant*. Gemma was watching the others. She could sense their disappointment.

'So – tell me about your pet – this Hobart,' she asked suddenly.

'He's our friend,' said Lincoln simply.

'He's like a member of the family,' said Gran. 'And you don't desert your family if they're in trouble, do you?'

'Never,' said Gemma.

'Well, that's how we feel about our Hobart,' said Simone, smiling.

'And we're going to find him, even if we have to get out and push the *Valiant*,' chirped Glenn. 'Right, Planet Man?'

The eyes lit up on the doll on the dashboard.

'Heroes – *Glenn* – brush their teeth in a firm, circular motion,' it said.

Gemma just stared at it. She licked her lips hungrily.

'You can't eat it,' Gran warned her.

'Unless you're really hungry,' whispered Simone.

'Object ahead.'

The two simple words cut through the air like a scalpel. Everyone turned to Lincoln, who had spoken. Then they looked at the windscreen. There were only stars ahead of them.

'I don't see anything,' said Simone.

'It's a stationary spacecraft. It should be visible in thirty-two universal seconds,' said Lincoln, busily processing data as it came in.

Suddenly, another shudder forced the Clarks to grab on to the nearest solid object and brace themselves.

'It's the number-one engine!' shouted Glenn. 'It's gone into shut-down!'

'I don't believe it!' cried Gran.

'It's all right,' said Lincoln calmly. 'Our momentum will carry us towards this object. It's not going anywhere.'

The *Valiant* kept coming. Silent, soundless.

'There!' cried Gemma, staring out the windscreen. A tiny point of light was visible in the distance. They were headed straight for it.

The point of light grew slowly. It got brighter, clearer – then individual features could be seen. Familiar features. The huge engines. The rows and rows of windows. The impressive superstructure that Glenn had stared at for days back on Old Earth until every detail was etched into his mind.

'It's the *Dogstar*!' cried Glenn.

'Boombah confirms that,' said Gran, pointing to the B-Cam. On it, Boombah was looking exhausted. But with the little strength he still possessed, he was clawing frantically at his glass covering, still trying feebly to get at the object in the distance.

'Poor Boombah,' sighed Simone. 'Isn't there anything you can do for him?'

'Yes,' said Lincoln. He pressed a button. Immediately, a bluish gas started floating into the nose-cone.

'This gas is a sense-deadening agent. It will overwhelm Boombah's nasal glands and render them effectively anaesthetised. He will be temporarily unable to smell anything else.'

Indeed, Boombah was already looking more relaxed. His nostrils stopped flaring. Sure enough, he yawned, stretched himself, then curled up for a nap, oblivious to the unfolding drama.

The *Valiant* was closing in on the *Dogstar*. Its size was minuscule compared to the giant Space Ark. It glided up alongside it – past the huge engines, past the rows and rows of windows. From each window, a dog's face peered out.

'Look at them,' said Glenn. 'Their tails are wagging!'

And, indeed, all of the dogs who saw the *Valiant* gliding past were excited. They hadn't seen a legitimate human for ages. Every single one of them was reminded of their homes at that moment.

'But why has the ship stopped?' asked Simone. 'Has it broken down? Is there something wrong with the pilots?'

'Pull alongside the cockpit,' suggested Lincoln to Glenn. 'Then fire the stabilizers.'

'I'm on to it,' replied Glenn.

Inside the *Dogstar*, Zeke and Alice were conscious that the dogs had started barking. A huge, joyous chorus of barks, yelps and howls, unlike anything they'd heard before, was coming from every deck of the ship. Listening to it, Hobart was getting excited, too. He started running around the cockpit, peering out the windows, trying to get a glimpse of what the dogs on the lower levels had seen.

'Why are they so excited, Zeke?' asked Alice.

'I've got no idea.'

Suddenly the intercom came alive with a voice. Simone's voice.

'*Valiant* to *Dogstar* – are you reading me, over?' she said.

Zeke and Alice jumped up immediately. Hearing the familiar voice, Hobart's ears pricked up. Could it be . . . ?

'*Dogstar* to *Valiant* – we can hear you,' replied Zeke. 'Where are you?'

Just then, a shadow started to engulf the cockpit. Zeke, Alice and Hobart looked out to see a rusty, beaten-up, singed and dented spaceship pulling up beside them.

'We're right here,' replied Simone.

That's Simone's voice! I know that voice! And there! It's the Valiant! Wuzza!

There's my pack! There's Glenn. Gran's waving. Simone looks like she's crying. And Lincoln's there, too. With another greeny-looking no-hair. Who's that?

Doesn't matter. They've come! They've come because they need me! Glenn needs a lather! Simone needs a walk! Lincoln needs me to guard his room! Yes!

I can do my job! Wuzza!

'Look at Hobart's tail wag!' yelled Glenn, pointing wildly into the cockpit as he brought the ship to a halt. 'I'll bring us closer . . .'

Deftly moving the *Valiant* with just the thruster-stabilizers, Glenn turned, pitched it over and rolled until the windows in the cockpit were right up next to the windows of the *Dogstar*'s cockpit.

Through them, the kids could see Hobart's tail wagging and his tongue hanging out happily. The Clarks all pressed up against the window, trying to get as close as they could to Hobart.

'Did you miss us?' said Simone, as if expecting Hobart could hear.

Hobart barked. All right – of course they couldn't hear it, but his mouth was moving and every one of them knew exactly what Hobart would be saying. He said the same thing every time they came home.

'He's saying he did miss us,' said Simone. And no one was about to argue with her this time.

The kids' faces were pressed up hard against the glass, when Zeke did something unexpected. He picked up Hobart and held him up in the cockpit.

Glenn pushed his hand up to the glass. Hobart tried to lick it.

'See that, Simone? He likes me better than you.'

'Huh! Hobart – give me paw,' said Simone.

Simone held out her hand to the window. As best they could, they bumped knuckles, rolled wrists, touched middle fingers, high-fived each other, then rubbed noses – well . . . glass.

'See that?' said Simone. 'He likes me better than you.'

Lincoln sighed. He pushed a button on Simone's radio and spoke: 'Hobart – rotate laterally and feign rigor mortis.'

Right on cue, Hobart rolled over and played dead. For a moment Zeke and Alice looked worried, but then Hobart jumped up happily and kept barking at the familiar faces.

'Oh – a joke,' said Zeke. 'Yes, we humans enjoy jokes! Hoh. Hoh. Most amusing.'

Alice looked from Hobart to the crew of the Valiant and back again. She wasn't programmed for a wide range of emotions, but happiness was one of them. She knew what she was seeing – but she also knew there was something more there.

'Who are you people?' she finally asked over the radio.

'We're Hobart's family,' declared Gran triumphantly.

'Oh. How wonderful. We're so glad you finally came. How did you find us?'

The Clarks exchanged looks.

'We just followed our noses,' said Glenn.

And hearing this, Hobart barked. A joyous yelp just like the first time they'd met. Glenn had just said something Hobart understood perfectly.

Puffin by Post

Dogstar – Philip Dalkin

If you have enjoyed this book and want to read more,
then check out these other great Puffin titles.
You can order any of the following books direct with Puffin by Post:

Give Peas a Chance • Morris Gleitzman • 9780141324111	£4.99
'A brilliantly funny writer' – *Sunday Telegraph*	

I, Nigel Dorking • Mary-Anne Fahey • 9780141323770	£5.99
Hilarious, moving and clever – if you like Adrian Mole, you'll love this!	

Diary of a Wimpy Kid • Jeff Kinney • 9780141324906	£4.99
Hilarious comic-style adventure and *New York Times* number-one bestseller – Captain Underpants meets *The Simpsons*!	

The BFG • Roald Dahl • 9780141322629	£5.99
Meet the Big Friendly Giant – an absolute classic from the world's favourite storyteller	

The Unluckiest Boy in the World • Andrew Norriss • 9780141318776	£4.99
'Norriss has a wonderful light comic touch' – *Sunday Telegraph*	

Just contact:

Puffin Books, C/o Bookpost, PO Box 29,
Douglas, Isle of Man, IM99 1BQ
Credit cards accepted. For further details:
Telephone: 01624 677237
Fax: 01624 670923

You can email your orders to: bookshop@enterprise.net
Or order online at: www.bookpost.co.uk

Free delivery in the UK.
Overseas customers must add £2 per book.

Prices and availability are subject to change.

Visit puffin.co.uk to find out about the latest titles, read extracts and exclusive author interviews, and enter exciting competitions.
You can also browse thousands of Puffin books online.